fagih@hotmail.com

WHO'S AFRAID OF AGATHA CHRISTIE? AND OTHER STORIES

Ahmed Fagih moves further into the world of contemporary English literature with this second collection of short stories under the Kegan Paul Imprint. Who's Afraid of Agatha Christie and Other Stories exemplifies Fagih's characteristic mixing of illusion and reality, his complexity of style, and his penchant for lyrical writing.

T0347437

WHO'S AFRAID OF AGATHA CHRISTIE? AND OTHER STORIES

TRANSLATED FROM THE ARABIC

AHMED FAGIH

Routledge
Taylor & Francis Group

LONDON AND NEW YORK

First published in 2000 by
Kegan Paul International

This edition first published in 2011 by
Routledge
2 Park Square, Milton Park, Abingdon, Oxfordshire OX14 4RN

Simultaneously published in the USA and Canada
by Routledge
711 Third Avenue, New York, NY 10017

First issued in paperback 2016

Routledge is an imprint of the Taylor & Francis Group, an informa business

British Library Cataloguing in Publication Data
A catalogue record for this book is available from the British Library

ISBN 13: 978-1-138-98713-5 (pbk)
ISBN 13: 978-0-7103-0632-6 (hbk)

Publisher's Note
The publisher has gone to great lengths to ensure the quality of this reprint
but points out that some imperfections in the original copies may be
apparent. The publisher has made every effort to contact original copyright
holders and would welcome correspondence from those they have been
unable to trace.

Who's Afraid of Agatha Christie? and other Stories

Contents

1

Who's Afraid of Agatha Christie?

I chose a well-lit place in the depth of the lobby and sat reading a translated detective story by Agatha Christie, to while away the time. I was panting with her words, following the crimes of an anonymous criminal, burning with curiosity to know the doer. I did not notice the man who came and sat next to me on the same sofa, in spite of the many vacant seats which filled the lobby of the hotel. He took me by surprise when he bent his head near me, contemplating the lines of the book I was reading. I raised my head looking at him with wonder. He smiled without the least feeling of embarrassment, fixing his eyes in the book, and asking me in English :

'It seems a strange language. Is it Sanskrit?'

'It is Arabic.'

I said that carelessly, without any desire to continue the conversation or interest in the lines of surprise which appeared on his forehead. I buried my face in the book looking for the line I stopped at, hoping the man had satisfied his curiosity and decided to leave me alone with my book. I felt his breath near me and his shoulder rubbing mine. He had bent his head contemplating the book anew. I closed the book angrily and looked at him deprecatingly asking him without words to go away. But the man wore that meaningless smile on his face, before saying :

'You are an Arab then.'

God give me strength! He did not want to spare me. And the world of the story which was full of criminal murders made me more cautious, made my mood more intense in the presence of intruders like him and there was nothing left for me but to leave the lobby and look for somewhere else.

'Yes I'm an Arab. And you?'

I do not know why I got involved in asking that question which opened the door for a conversation I could not bring to an end. Perhaps I wanted to know to which nationality that inquisitive animal belonged and why he chose me in particular to be his company that evening. He said with a laugh :

'I'm a hybrid.'

I was satisfied with the word which does not mean anything

1

except that he was a cut off human being, without origin or roots. Actually his appearance did not suggest that he belonged to any race in particular. I nodded thanking him, as if to tell him that was all I wanted to know. I went back to the book searching for the murder between the lines. He lit a cigarette, inhaled a deep breath, then puffed its smoke in the air. I started pushing the clouds of smoke away, beating the air with my hand nervously and convulsively, whereas he carried on the conversation indifferent to the revulsion I showed.

'My mother is a negress who emigrated from Africa, and my father is an Irish emigrant. They met in Costa Rica when they were working on the tobacco plantations. So tobacco is in my blood. I sucked it with my mother's milk. Would you like a cigarette?'

'No, thank you.'

What a nice lineage, I thought. Perhaps he would be satisfied with that much explanation. I did not have time to listen to his life story, soaked in the mud of tobacco plantations. I was tracking down a very cunning murderer, and had to find him out among all those suspects who filled the world of the story, and that Costa Rican gentleman was making my task more difficult.

'I'm Costa Rican by birth only. I am all the time emigrating. Honduras. Peru. Colombia. Bermuda. They are all my countries by residence. For emigrating is part of my nature. It is the heritage I carry in my blood.'

I had to re-read the page anew, or else I would lose the threads which would lead me to the murderer. I would not let that man who had been raised in tobacco plantations and who was fond of changing homelands as people do with their socks, deprive me of the pleasure of looking for the murderer and finding him out. The writer had put in my way a criminal – a drug addict, who worked as a mediator between prostitutes and pleasure seekers, that I might be persuaded that he was the murderer, whereas the real murderer would not be expected to be the great benefactor who set up hospitals and made donations to orphanages. It was only a hunch. I still needed more evidence to pass a decisive judgement convicting him.

'I have come to Malta on some business of the charity society which I have the honour to be a member of. It is a society which takes interest in the victims of loneliness and depression, and it is sponsored by the Catholic Church. We are going to set up a branch here.'

My head was filled with the ringing of bells of the fire brigades, the beat of the horses' hooves the cavaliers of Saint John of Malta rode on their invasions. Here were charitable and pious men dominating the world of detective stories just as they were jostling me in the lobbies of first-class hotels. The man had seen me sitting alone, abstinent from the clamour of a boisterous night life of the island, and thought with the ethics of a knight of the Middle Ages that I was one of the victims of depression who needed the care of his charitable society. But I was sure that what summoned him to my place was nothing but the characters of the novel who admired the analogy between themselves and the qualities of the man. Hence they used the power of imagination to exercise control over my reality, fetched that man from the farthest parts of the globe and landed him on my seat. He had put out his cigarette, and my nerves calmed down a little. I contemplated him while he was still wearing his smiling mask, trying to find out the common denominators between him and the characters of the novel. He was almost sixty years old, with brown complexion and tiny features, endowed by old age with delicacy and fineness and a touch of familiarity and friendliness. He was wearing a white, elegant jacket and a decorated shirt which indicated youthfulness of heart. On his wrist he wore a watch emanating the colour of gold, evidence of richness and welfare. Had I met him at any other time, away from this detective story, which filled my head with frightening imaginings, I would have liked his meek appearance and found comfort in his company.

'My name is Alberto.'

He extended his hand to shake mine. I placed my hand in his and withdrew it without mentioning my name. I had already decided to leave the place and move with my book to another place. Before I stood up, she came running, fluttering with her bare arms and her full, dancing breasts. She was wearing a summer blouse and jeans. I figured out she was his daughter. But he introduced her to me saying :

'Rosetta, my wife. She is a hybrid like me.'

What I saw was something that did not belong except to a beautiful, wonderful world, more joyful than our world, a world from which thieves and killers had disappeared together with loneliness and depression. That smile which carried a promise, an omen and a joy, and those wide eyes which occupied half the face and sent out rays penetrating into the heart were but a sign of the birth of a new, beautiful world. I sat stunned, my eyes glued to her, melting in the magic of her presence. Her body was the incarnation of femininity in the glory of its triumph and explosiveness. The face

3

was painted with a brush soaked in the colours of the horizon at day-break, glowing and shining, as if the woman had just landed from the solar boats. I neglected the book with its dark worlds which dealt with the darkest areas of human psyche. I started blaming myself because I made that book a reference and a guide to knowing the human beings around me. My feelings opened up like the sunflower when the rays of the planet which illumines the universe fall on it. My joy was mixed with some sorrow as I wondered why my luck was always that sad. Why did I always meet the woman who set fire to my blood except in the company of other men who had preceded me to her and made a barrier between us. She occupied a chair in front of us and went on talking to her husband about the shop of antiquities annexed to the hotel, inviting him to go with her, perhaps they might find something to buy as a keepsake. He convinced her to go to the store on her own under the pretence that he was busy talking to me. After she had gone he addressed me saying :

'We are husband and wife without marriage, that is without any official contracts or church ceremonies. No doubt you know something about the strictness of the Catholic Church. Therefore I left my first wife without divorce and married Rosetta without marriage. And we are happy with this nice arrangement.'

I did not know why I felt some relief when he said that, as if their companionship without marriage removed an ethical fetter and freed me from the embarrassment I experienced as I felt my heart go for a married woman.

'I haven't had the honour of knowing your name.'

'Samy.'

I said the name without any hesitation this time but I had perverted Ismail for Samy.

'It is an easy name to pronounce. Samy we shall be friends.'

I did not tell him I was leaving the following day or that my presence in Malta was nothing but the consequence of an emergency as the aeroplane which brought me to the airport of the island was late for the take-off of another aeroplane which was taking me back to my city. So the airline company had lodged me in this five-star hotel which I had never dreamt to be one of its lodgers one day. And because I was penniless, and had no money to frequent night clubs I gallivanted for a while in the streets and in that lobby to while away the time reading that detective story.

I was still too embarrassed to ask him for the reason which made him leave the other seats and choose to sit next to me. But he spared me the trouble when he said, as if he was reading my mind,

'Perhaps you wonder why I came and sat beside you. You looked strange, sitting all by yourself in this luxurious hotel which is full of night clubs, and dancing and gambling casinos, reading a book. A tourist does not come to Malta to do this, because he can stay at home if he wants to read. I thought you were waiting for a friend. But when I left the hotel and came back more than an hour later, to find you still reading this book, I realised at once that you are a rare man, an exceptional man who could rescue himself from the rat race and retain his distinctive character above imitating the others and following in their footsteps. I immediately remember St Augustine. My long service in our society provided me with an insight which enables me to recognise unique human beings, who live in their spiritually rich world. So, I wanted to get to know you.'

I thanked him for his penetrating insight, which possessed the power to communicate with the saints and count me one of them. But why did he break through this private world which he saw I was enjoying? Should I have told him that the world he took to be a spiritual, unique world as nothing but the world of empty pockets which urged me to imprison myself in that lobby keeping company with the killers and criminals who inhabit the world of Agatha Christie. Should I have told him that I could not care less for him or the transparence of his insight, but for that female loaded with the storms and volcanoes of the Andes mountains and the savagery of the Amazon forests she came from, who forced me to forsake my private world to break through her world. I was confirmed in my belief that he could read minds, when he said,

'What do you think of Rosetta. Don't tell me you're not infatuated with her beauty, because this is what she does with all people. All of them fall victims of her love at first sight. Isn't that what happened to you too?'

What could I say. He had expressed my feelings in a way I could not express. I was but one of her victims, no doubt. And as he had dressed me in the cassocks of St Augustine, my confessions should not have been less frank than his own. I said :

'Yes. This is what happened to me. And you should excuse me for this. For she has that kind of beauty which deserves to be worshipped.'

Then I put my hand on his shoulder, as if to ask for his forgiveness for what I said, saying :

'You're a lucky man, very lucky, my friend, for the gods have bestowed her on you and nobody else.'

I did not know what came over me. I remained stunned, silent,

5

looking in the vacuum, motionless, when I heard him say, without preparation or alarm :

'Wouldn't you like to host her in your bed tonight?'

The statement was a strong slap on my face, which made me unaware of the world for a minute or more. I could not bring myself to believe that the woman was an article for sale and purchase, and that the man was a trader selling her charm and beauty to the clients of first-class hotels. Agatha Christie's book was still in my hand, its lines telling the story of the brokers of sex, exerting pressure on my memory at that moment, as if they were pointing to that strange compatibility between what was happening in the novel and what was happening then.

What could I tell him now? His sitting next to me was only part of the plan he laid to catch me. His talk about churches, saints and charity societies was nothing but a beautiful cover, in which he covered himself up to make people feel at ease with him, before he revealed his true identity. No doubt he knew I was an Arab, and took me for one of the rich Arabs, when he saw me residing in a first-class hotel. His experiences must have taught him that Arabs were more generous when the matter involved a woman of Rosetta's qualification.

I had regained my equilibrium after his excellent offer.

'And what is the price you exact in return?'

I wanted to use from the start a language which agreed with the language of his profession.

'All that we want is to make you happy.'

This is what the masters of blackmail say all over the world. They abstain from naming the price under the pretext that their aim is nothing but to make you happy. I wished I could pretend to be stupid and believe he favoured me with that precious gift as a result of his admiration for me and his desire to make a man suffering from loneliness and depression like myself happy, and take her to my room, host her in my bed without somebody asking me to pay the price.

At that moment Rosetta had returned with a pendant of blue beads in her hand, expressing her admiration for it and asking her imaginary husband what he thought of it. He took the pendant from her twirling it before his eyes, and praising Rosetta's taste. Then, turning to me, he added :

'Rosetta believes in luck, believes that blue beads bring good luck.'

He returned the pendant to her saying :

6

'Our friend Samy admires you. He wants to spend the night in your company. What do you think?'

'Whatever you say, dear.'

'He is asking about the price. I told him there's no price for love, because it is not a matter of buying and selling.'

The woman smiled coyly, then said :

'Yes, dear Alberto. The whole world is worth nothing without love.'

Then she added, raising her eyes towards me :

'I like him. He's a nice person. He likes reading books. Look at him. He's still holding the book with his finger between the pages, afraid of losing the last line at which he stopped.'

Alberto put out his hand to take the book from me.

'See? Rosetta loves you, and is jealous of the book for you. Let us fold this page this way. You can go back to it tomorrow.'

He folded the page and returned the book to me, saying :

'There's no longer a place for me between you. I'll go to my room now, and see you tomorrow. Have good fun both of you.'

Alberto went away leaving me alone with that hybrid woman of the Andes mountains. It was not possible that this breath-taking beauty, this divine banquet loaded with all sorts of pleasures and joy, to be monopolised by one man in the world, especially if that man was concerned, like Alberto about the grief of human beings afflicted with loneliness and depression like me. He knew that a treatment like that would ensure immediate and effective cure. I wanted to ask Rosetta about the secret of her relationship with that man who lived on selling her flesh on the market. But I found it a needless question, which would not add fresh knowledge to me, and it might upset her. Those were the rules of the market. The broker had done his piece of work and would collect his reward after the conclusion of the deal. There was nothing left for me but to know the price so that I could withdraw with dignity, as if my withdrawal came as an objection to the principle of exploitation and not my inability to pay the price. Before I could ask the question, she volunteered to answer saying in slow sentences, separated by moments of silence, contemplation and fiddling with the blue beads.

'Alberto discerned magnanimity in you since he knew you were an Arab.'

My intuition was right then. He did not come to sit beside me except after he had completed his investigations about me. Rosetta stopped talking for a while, as she raised her profuse eyelashes to me and fixed her large eyes directly into my eyes. She had no need

7

to use all those weapons on me for I had declared my complete surrender since I saw her, and raised before her the white flag, evidence of my helplessness and defeat.

'He realised it was you who would get us out of our dilemma.'

Yes. Yes. So begin all the pleasant stories of picaroons who are full of tricks and deceit. I made a bet she would talk about the money stolen by thieves or appropriated by the owners of gambling tables, who took advantage of the innocence of customers who went to watch and be entertained.

'We spent last night in the gambling casino of this hotel and without knowing it we found ourselves losing all our money. You may not believe that we are now unable to pay for the cost of our stay at the hotel which has lasted for more than two weeks.'

Here she was confirming my intuition once more. I was sure she knew that I too knew that what she was saying was a faked up tale. But the exorbitant price she was asking for, needed also the cover of beautiful imagination to erase from it the crudeness and the vulgarity.

I admired her ability of faking up the tale, and felt sorry I did not possess money to rescue her from her imaginary dilemma and buy for myself a love night with her. I remembered I was not the victim of their deceit. It was I who deceived them by being in that five-star hotel, until they thought I was one of the wealthy who could buy those heavenly banquets. So I would continue the game of deceit, but this time I would play it with myself. I would fight the surge of blood in my veins which yearned for a moment of engagement with her blood and veins. I shall claim before myself that I loathe her and I do not want to sleep with her, because she is a vulgar woman selling herself in the markets of human flesh. I knew I was lying to myself, and that my lust for her, which was not fulfilled that night, would leave a deep sorrow which would never be quenched in my heart. I would use Agatha Christie and her world of criminals in that game of deceit. I would open the book and look for the page at which I stopped to make her believe I was averse to concluding the deal with her. I saw her look at me wondering, as I opened the book, so I said with a smile :

'It is an exciting detective story.'

Her face clouded and her fingers convulsed as she held the blue beads. She asked me passionately :

'What did you say?'

'I said it is a story by Agatha Christie full of suspense and mystery.'

8

'I mean what do you say to what I told you?'

'It is really a dilemma. I honestly wish I could help you but ...'

'But what? Didn't you say you wanted to spend some time with me?'

'I wish I could be your bridegroom even for one hour, but I need a whole year to save the dowry you ask for.'

'It is not your fault. It is the fault of Alberto who always involves me in these damned situations.'

Then she added springing up from her seat angrily :

'I wish you an enjoyable evening in the company of Agatha Christie.'

With quick steps she left the lobby. Rosetta was gone taking away with her the fragrance of her femininity and the lustre of her smile, and I was left alone with Agatha Christie and her dark worlds which are full of mysterious murders.

2

The Night of the Masks

He entered the ceremony hall, wearing the mask of a donkey. The administration of the tourist village had included in its programme a night entitled the night of the masks and exhibited in the shop of the village varied and various numbers of masks to provide the guests of the party with a wide range of choice.

He went to the shop some hours before the time appointed for the ceremony. He stood in the middle of the forest of masks trying to find a mask to his taste. He tried the mask of the lion and found it too tight, exerting pressure on his temples, chin and forehead. He looked at his face in the mirror. He saw his eyes transform into part of the lion's features. He discovered they did not suit the dignity of the king of the forest and despite the ferocity of its canine teeth, the density of the hair which surrounds the face of the lion and the aptness of the design of the rest of the features, those two eyes are what make a lion a lion. The same with the tiger, whose eyes seemed less lustrous when he wore its mask and looked through the eyes of that animal which resembled a burning arrow. He made sure that he was not fit for the role of one of the forest leaders, and had to look for himself for a modest place among the members of the subjects. Before he could bring his choice a little lower to the categories which constitute the lowest rung of the social ladder of the forest creatures, he thought of trying his luck with the hawk. It is a generous, noble bird; that loves freedom and is enamoured of high peaks. Such a mask was worthy of granting him a sense of prestige and would enable him to overcome and do away with the embarrassment he always feels in such merry-making parties. But when he looked at his face in the mirror and saw the long, pointed peak and the area of the narrow eyes, he realised to what extent the mask was out of harmony with the rest of his physique. With a feeling of sorrow he replaced the mask and went on contemplating the rest of the masks hanging down in the shop. He let alone the horned animals and did not go near the bull, the reindeer or the he-goat, including the unicorn. He did not want to walk around wearing one or two horns on his head. But he did not hesitate to try on many others like the horse, the dog, the cat, the wolf, the rabbit, the

11

monkey, the bear and the hyena. He put them all on his face.

He contemplated his image in the mirror, and asked the shop girl what she thought of them. She was not happy with the way he looked. He was not happy either. He saw other masks of frogs, mice, lizards and squirrels and did not go near them, because he did not want to belong to their world. He went to a stall which contained masks inspired by animation films and their figures like Mickey Mouse, Donald Duck and the seven pigs. He found them commonplace, old-fashioned. They did not excite his curiosity. He stood perplexed. His eyes went reviewing the exhibition of the animal faces, while he was laughing at himself and at the idea of that party which he had never experienced before, asking himself if it was wise to be party to a masquerade of that sort, if it suited young people under twenty, it was not suitable for a middle-aged man like him. He wanted to leave the shop and give up the idea of participating in that kind of masquerade, when he caught sight of the mask of the donkey, as he was heading for the door, blocking his way. He came to a halt to reconsider, looking at the mask. He remembered the relationship which attached him to this animal when he was young and had never left the village. He saw with his mind's eye that old, lean donkey which shared residence with them inside the house and was treated like a member of the family. This called to memory the errands he went on in the company of the donkey to the forest of palm trees outside the village or to the fields of melons, when he came back with it loaded with dates, melons or firewood, while he topped the load, humming and singing, and the donkey trotting happily as if it were dancing. Some sort of companionship started between him and that donkey, until he started personally to undertake offering it food and water. When the donkey fell seriously ill as a result of senility, they took him to the desert to meet his fate as prey to beasts. He knew what happened, and for days on end he kept crying in the night, asking his family passionately about the destiny of the donkey after death, whether donkeys also went to paradise. For he saw that this kind, patient and struggling animal was the worthiest of all creatures to go to the paradise of God.

The shop girl saw him stand for a long time in front of the donkey's mask, and extended her hand to offer him the mask and help him fix it on his face. As soon as he put it on, he felt that that mask was exactly what he was looking for. He asked the shop girl for her opinion and she showed great enthusiasm for the face of the donkey. She saw it became him more than any other animal. The mask was comfortable. The large features of the face of the donkey were spacious and expansive and did not exert any pressure on his ears, eyes, nose and mouth as the case was with the other masks. They allowed him to see, hear, breathe and talk without the least trouble. When he looked at his face in the mirror, he admired the symmetry between the donkey's face and his outer appearance, as if his physique was never created except to suit the donkey's face. There was no room for hesitation. That mask made him more enthusiastic to participate in such a funny party, which would be satiric of human life and a glorification of the world of beasts and insects. He bought the mask, waited for the appointed time for the party, wore it and entered the spacious hall to which a large number of mask wearers had preceded him. He discovered that he was in the middle of a forest full of various shapes of animals. He cast a look at the décor of the hall, saw tall trees made of cardboard climbing the walls with branches of light hanging down from them and felt he was entering a magical forest.

Everything in the forest looked in harmony with the spirit of the party, including its organiser, who looked like one of the fairies of the forest. She wore round her neck flower wreaths, stuck red and white roses in her fair plaits of hair and wore a dress which resembled the wing of butterflies encircled by phosphorous rings which made it twinkle and gleam. She kept her face uncovered to distinguish herself from the rest of the participants who covered their faces with masks and wore ordinary evening dresses and so it became easy for him to distinguish the gentlemen from the ladies.

The organiser of the party was holding a microphone in her hand, asking the participants to avoid speaking the human language and to emit sounds in keeping with the masks they wore. The place resounded with the croaking of frogs, the neighing of horses, the roaring of lions, the howling of wolves, the barking of dogs, the mewing of cats, the bleating of sheep, the bellowing of bulls and the cries of monkeys. He found he had to bray like a donkey.

He remained mute for a short while, in an attempt to get over the embarrassment he felt. He had chosen to wear the mask of a donkey but to assimilate its feelings and behaviour and bray like it seemed an extremely difficult task. He discovered that his appearance as he stood silent excited surprise in the eyes of his fellow inhabitants of the forest. He started to bray in a low key. He liked the game, felt the pleasure of entering into the atmosphere of the party and raised his voice braying as loudly as the donkeys in his village. He discovered there were others braying like him, men and women wearing the same mask of the donkey. He felt comfort as he was not the only donkey in the party.

The forest fairy was fluttering her wings in the lights, holding the microphone, congratulating the participants on excelling in their parts and their outstanding ability to metamorphose from their human nature to their animal nature which they had acquired only a few moments ago and calling upon each and every one of them to forget his profession, education, social status, his or her native country and to be in full harmony with the spirit, temperament and character of the mask he or she was wearing. She did not want to see human beings that evening, but the forest animals enjoying and celebrating the peace achieved among their conflicting factions. But the conflict had not disappeared for good on the land of the forest. For there were the males going round the females as the males of the forest do with its females, skirmishing. Here was a lion at odds with another lion over a woman wearing the mask of a lioness, and there was a monkey jostling another over a woman wearing the mask of the monkey clan. But it was the kind of skirmishing which was satisfied with roaring and shouting and never reached the point of fighting or engaging with canine teeth and claws, in observance of the rules of the game and the principle of peace achieved by the forest inmates.

He also tried to find a she-donkey to chase and bray a little in the face of the donkey going round her, and because he did not find one near at hand to play with, he made his way in the crowd looking for her. Before he could reach her, he saw a woman wearing the mask of a cat. He knew at once that she was the same woman he had seen leaving the shop of masks carrying the same mask. He had seen her before and noticed her feminine qualifications which planted in his heart trees of fire. Two full breasts preceding her, two full lips separated by a small aperture as if they were in a state of readiness to receive kisses and a swinging body emanating a frank invitation to the game of love.

On one of the hop evenings he tried to follow her and win a dance with her. He broke through the siege laid around her by admirers of her beauty until he reached her but he met with repulse. Perhaps those admirers would not notice her tonight or discover her identity behind the guise of that mask, and he would enjoy a night of love with her. He had not come on that vacation or joined that caravan of tourists who ended up in this tourist village except to look for an escapade provided by the tolerance of relationships in these foreign cities to recompense for the days of drought and dryness he lived amidst the traditions of his desert city, which takes pride in wearing the mask of virtue and segregates men and women.

But how could he overleap the barriers imposed by nature between cats and donkeys. He wished he had gone back to the shop, when he saw her buying the mask of the cat and bought a mask similar to hers. Then it would have been easier for him to win her company for the night. The game had its rules. How could he tamper with those rules which stood between him and her. He realised he was actually a donkey and not only by virtue of the mask.

The organiser of the party had found the time suitable for dancing. They had passed the first test when they did away with the language of human beings in favour of the language of howling, braying and roaring. She called upon them to go through the second test by which they confirmed their belonging to the animal kingdom. She entered the dancing ring, and with the help of music and the circle of light which followed her and the phosphorous matter in her dress, she was transformed into a butterfly of fire fluttering with her arms and dancing as if she were flying in the air. She invited the attendants to dance like her, dances in keeping with the masks they wore. The lion had to perform the dance which suited lions, and similarly the deer, the bulls, the monkeys and the hawks. People started to beat the air with their feet, heads and hands, jumping like monkeys, swimming in the air with arms like birds' wings, beating the ground with their hooves like horses. He found himself in the middle of a wave lifting him up and hurling him in the middle of the dance ring. He kept raising his head upwards to smell the air, imitating the donkey in its state of excitation when it kicks the ground, beats the air with its hooves, ecstatic with the freedom the donkey's mask afforded him, kicking, running loose, trampling on others' feet and being trampled on. Nothing mattered. He was enjoying this animal nature which afforded him the chance without fearing any blame for being ignorant of the rules of dancing.

The band went on playing their music which resembled howling, and the lights continued to come from the ceiling of the hall in circles and quick flashes. Their outpouring endowed the movement of the dancers with more excitement. He continued his beastly dancing, braying every now and then whenever a woman came near him swinging her breasts and hips in her imitation of the dance of sows. He felt tired and left the dance ring. He sat aside panting, wiping the sweat oozing from his neck and chest, trying to locate the woman wearing the cat's mask after he had lost sight of her while he was dancing. He wandered in the corners of the hall looking for her.

15

He discovered there were small rooms next to the hall, sparsely lit, full of comfortable sofas and chairs, on which a number of the companions in the party sat in pairs, men and women, chattering, embracing and sometimes taking off their masks to kiss each other without any commitment to the instructions of the announcer or to the fact that the male should accompany a woman of his own species. For he saw in those rooms the lion in the company of a bitch, the bull hugging a lizard, the unicorn in the company of a giraffe, the wolf wooing a chicken and the reindeer speaking softly to the sow. He was a donkey when he thought the forest had a law. The forest overleaps all rules and laws. That was, then, his chance to be alone with that cat which enchanted his mind and heart and take sips from the glass of her beauty and femininity to the point of fulfilment. He could not reach her with the methods of human beings. He would try to reach her with the methods of the forest creatures. He looked for her, without caring this time for the talk of the announcer who went in instigating the participants to assimilate their roles and tempting them with a grand prize dedicated to the winner who excels the others with his cleverness in impersonating and imitating the animal whose mask he had chosen to wear. He saw his cat jumping among the dancers and mewing seductively and sexually. He walked until he reached her. He went on dancing and braying beside her, petting and frolicking with her, trying to make her feel at ease with him. The music slowed down, and with it the movements of the dancers became slower. He saw in this a chance for a slow dance with her. He encircled her with his arms, stuck his body to hers and leant his head on hers. He felt her pushing him away, trying to release her body from his grip to go back to her quick step. But he clung closer to her, careful to keep her in his embrace. Her whole body convulsed as he kept a firm hold on her body forbidding her to resist. He kept on dancing with her against her will, pushing her in the meantime towards the room next to the hall. When they reached the room he pulled her forcefully to the sofa. While she was still resisting and protesting he compelled her to sit on the sofa and he fell in a heap beside her apologising for the crude way he had treated her. He had something important to tell her and because he could find no other way amidst the noise and howling had been driven to take such drastic action. Before he started relating his important speech, she stood up angry, damning and swearing, looking for someone to throw him out of the party. She excited his anger, and he held her arm and threw her back on the sofa forcefully to prevent her from escaping, he fell on her, asking

16

her to listen to what he had to say, to afford him the chance of a moment of intimacy with her. She sent out loud cries which made the attendants hurry to her rescue and co-operate to haul him from above her. He had realised the atrocity of his deed and stood embarrassed, speechless. How could he justify the act and defend himself against her accusation of his attempted rape? Would it concede for him to say that he was only frolicking and playing with her as happens in animation films? Or would he tell them that he was carried away in his role in response to the rules of the game and the instructions of the superintendents of the party. Hence they had no right to blame him if he mastered his role, assimilated the feelings of the donkey and was overtaken by the animal lust which occur to donkeys.

He had been a donkey and because he had no handsome face, a sweet sound or an intelligent mind to take pride in among the forest inhabitants, he had used the only thing he excelled in among the rest of the creatures, his phallus.

He felt extreme panic as they were pulling him by the arm, leading him to the platform, exposing him under the brilliant lights, while the hall was overwhelmed with silence, expectation and waiting. He was sure they would expose him in front of the attendants, condemn his outrageous conduct which would lead him to court and years of imprisonment in keeping with the crime of rape. To his great astonishment they put a trophy in his hand, hung a wreath of flowers round his neck, declaring his name as the first winner of the contest whose conduct harmonised with the mask he was wearing. He was worthy of the title of the first animal that evening.

3

Don't Kill the Dog

I made up my mind in that instant that the people who thronged the large square, whether crowding inside the shops rising high on all sides, or just window-shopping, or who frequented the snack bars dotted here and there, consuming quick dispirited meals then hurrying along, were in fact all decent people who like doing good and were endeavouring to earn a respectable living. I decided that none amongst them was a thief, a killer or a scoundrel; none belonged to a gang of thugs or murderers. Even if one of them was guilty of a misdemeanour, I was certain that it was committed a long time ago in a moment of rashness without malice or forethought, and that by now he or she regretted their action and were determined to spend the rest of their lives respectably and honourable, not harming any one.

Now, somehow, I felt a bond of affection with them all. It was as if I had known each one of them personally, and that I would be able to walk up to any one of them and greet him or her by name, as if we had grown up together in the same neighbourhood, but lack of time prevented me from approaching them all, and reminding them of the close ties of friendship which had bound us together in the past, I decided in that moment to select one person from amongst them, whether man or woman, to be my friend for the rest of the day, which was my first in that city as a tourist.

I felt drawn to a middle-aged woman who stood beside a clothes shop, wearing a coat in spite of the mildness of the weather and carrying a basket full of vegetables. I could begin by asking her the way to the public library, an enquiry which would inspire confidence and increase a person's standing in the regard of these people. It would also gain their immediate admiration, for here was one person out of all this crowd rushing around to earn a living and to satisfy their material needs; or merely occupied with clothes, food, or cheap amusements, who still obeyed the call of the intellect and sought out places of learning and knowledge. This would present a suitable opening for striking up a conversation with this virtuous lady who, despite her age, still retained a trace of quiet beauty and who had to support four children since her husband had fallen prey to alcoholism and was unable to keep a job. Thus I immediately endowed her with a noble aim in life, but my curiosity to know more about her was extinguished as soon as I had invented that story for her. I would wait a while before making my choice, for in truth it was not the right time just then to engage in idle chatter with elderly people. Conversation with them was only pleasant sitting by fireplaces in modest hotels or back-street cafes on chilly winter days.

Now, during this beautiful weather, the atmosphere charged with the most exquisite perfumes, the hubbub emanating from the depth of the square and rising to the dome of the sky, the shop signs, the colours and the lights – all these things awakened in the heart a desire to embrace life in all its renewed verdant cycle, reflected in faces full of freshness and radiance. Therefore, I decided to enter one of those large stores – the most opulent, exciting and with the best décor – and start talking to one of the salesgirls. I would choose the most attractive and alluring and approach her, even if she was selling fur coats, I would pretend that I had a girlfriend with a similar build and measurements. I would ask her to try on one of the coats for me, then I would pay the price, leave it for her and depart forever. If she was selling rings I would pretend that the fingers of the one I love were similar to hers in softness and slenderness. If she was selling perfumes, I would ask her to select for me the most exclusive brand, I would then buy the ring or perfume or fur coat, present it to her and leave, not caring whether it would cost me all the travellers cheques I had. I would cut my trip short and return quite content, suffice it that I had created a lasting impression upon that girl and behaved in a manner reminiscent of a noble knight in bygone days of legends and black orchids.

I wanted that day to leave a momentous and great impression upon a beautiful woman.

I changed my mind about approaching the salesgirls and crossed the road to the opposite side for I had spotted a young woman, a lady, it was obvious that she was an employee of a ministry, or perhaps a teacher, or a laboratory researcher. Her countenance was severe and grave, her features aristocratic. Her firm steps indicated clearly that she had a definite planned destination in mind. I was struck by the roundness of her mouth. I resolved to offer her my companionship that day.

I realised from the start that I had set myself a difficult target which would test my ability, and that I must now pay particular attention to choosing a suitable opening gambit for striking up a conversation with this woman, who appeared not to have the time nor the inclination for a quick chat-up on a street corner. The technique of asking such a woman the way to the public library would not work as she would merely nod her head in the opposite direction and continue along her way. I know this type of woman, she would not welcome small talk at such a time of day. The best time to commence a friendship with her would be when she took her dog for walk in one of the public parks.

A woman with such demeanour gave the impression of belonging to the upper classes, and anyone with such a serious expression undoubtedly had a dog kept somewhere at home.

I wished that she had brought him along, my task would have been a hundred times easier. I would have immediately addressed the dog, praising his intelligence and beauty, as a prelude to a close friendship with her. But what did it matter. Why not invent a dog for her at this very moment and address him in order to commence this relationship which would doubtless be the source of great happiness for us both.

I had by now overtaken her, so I slowed down until she was level with me. I turned towards her and feigned amazement :

'My God, what a lovely dog!'

In truth I was looking at her mouth.

I saw her turn her head to the left and to the right, thinking I was addressing someone else. When she realised there was no one else around, she looked at me in surprise and quickened her steps. I matched her pace, my eyes travelling down her firm body until they reached her legs.

'What do you call this splendid dog?'

Her features grew even more severe and she scowled as she looked around but saw no dog.

'What dog are you talking about?!'

I had forced her to speak!

'Why, Miss, the one you're leading. I honestly like this breed of dogs very much. I have an aversion to large dogs ever since I was bitten by one as a child. I still have the traces of his teeth on my leg to this day! Still I am sure that this pretty little thing with his soft luxurious hair would not harm anybody, especially those Pekinese dogs, how I like them!'

I did not sense her recoiling, and glimpsed a slight tremor on her lips as if she was trying to suppress a smile. However, she continued to hurry along, almost in a trot. I wished she would slow down a little so that I could pick up the dog and hold him against my chest and run my fingers through his thick soft imaginary hair.

Although she did not slacken her pace, I bent down and scooped up the dog in a swift dextrous movement and held him against my chest, which made me very pleased with myself.

'What a nice friendly dog he is! I'm sure you take great pains to train him correctly, otherwise he would not display these admirable qualities.'

I parted and lifted the hair which hung over his eyes, smoothing it against his temples. The dog appeared at ease with the tone of my voice as if I had been his friend for a long time. His expression relaxed and he seemed content with my fondling. This in turn infected her own features, which relaxed too as I resumed talking to the dog:

'What a playful mischievous boy you are! I should leave your hair hanging over your brow and eyes. A romantic film star! I bet you charm and bewitch all the lovely lady dogs around! I know you, you little rascal...'

I was aware that she was watching me intently and decided now was the right moment to address her directly :

'You haven't told me yet, what do you call this handsome fellow?'

Perhaps it was the sight of some children crossing the road just then, laughing and skipping merrily, which tempted her to participate in the game. She quickly answered :

'Confucius!'

We had really begun playing the game now!

I was sorry that she had bestowed the name of such an eminent Chinese philosopher on this insignificant puny dog, with no value, brains or intelligence, not even a good pedigree. I placed Confucius back on the pavement. She was a woman of some intelligence, otherwise she would have used a more familiar Chinese name currently being mentioned on television news.

Confucius wagged his tail happily.

'It's a nice name.'

I said this flatteringly, and judged now was the time to take the game one step further, before this accused dog turns on me.

'He needs to go for a run in one of the nearby parks instead of walking in this large crowded square. It's a shame to waste such a lovely day and not let him romp on the grass. Let me hold his lead.'

I took the lead over and headed for the park without waiting for an answer from her.

I would not have been annoyed had she gone on her way and

decided not to follow me. I would then have considered the game at an end and this would not have affected my love or my feeling of universal friendship.

To my great surprise she followed me and unhesitatingly, not even stopping for a moment to reconsider or show reluctance as most women usually did in similar situations. I started to lead the dog in steps akin to dancing, indeed I was dancing! I decided then that I was in love with this magnificent female and that I would love her loyally. I was ready to prostrate myself on the ground and kiss her dainty feet with no sense of humiliation or degradation. The whole universe seemed even more radiant and glorious and the people who crowded the streets grew more handsome, beautiful and noble. Pekinese dogs were the most splendid breed in the world!

We arrived at the park in the twinkling of an eye and I was aware of the trees as noble beings – awesome, majestic, towering overhead and overwhelming. I saluted them in reverence and intimidation. The grass was green, moist and tender, covering the face of the earth in its maternal majesty. I lifted my gaze up towards the thin spring clouds drifting across the face of the sky, and sensed that God was watching and blessing me. I waved back, smiling. My senses were extra sharp and my disposition serene. I was confronted by a red carnation but despite warning notices, I picked it and offered it to my lady as a token of love and loyalty. We sat down together on the green carpet. There were other people in the park exercising their dogs. I unleashed Confucius and urged him to run free over the grass, thanking him for the favour he did me in being the means of introduction to this lady, for without him I would not have dared aspire to get even a word from her. The dog ran wild over the green earth. I thought of asking her name, what kind of work she did and the destination she was heading for when we met, but I decided against this. I realised that these were but meaningless questions and a detraction from this moment in all its magic and beauty. Names were but mere symbols. I decided to grant her a name to call her by – a name chosen by me alone and not by some elderly relative of hers. I wanted it to be a lovely unusual name symbolising the spirit of the moment.

I pondered for a few minutes then hit on the name 'Venus'. That was to be her name from now on and I was but a worshipper at the altar of her beauty! She laughed when I told her this but continued to follow the dog with her eyes. I wanted to share her interest in him so I asked :

'How old is he?'

'What do you think?'

I had no experience with dogs or their ages or how long they lived.

In fact I wasn't fond of dogs and could not understand the kind of relationship that some people had with them. They were a compensation for the disappointment at the failure to maintain real friendship between people. There was something lacking in the lives of all these people who brought their dogs to the park, for in reality they were desperately lonely and I felt genuinely sorry for them.

'Perhaps he's five years old.'

'He's just one year old.'

'What a clever dog he is! I can't remember being able to run like this when I was a year old!'

Confucius had seen a ball land on the grass and chased after it, nudging it with his head towards us.

'I don't think anyone could have picked that ball up and run off with it so expertly when he was a year old! The development of dogs certainly is superior to that of human beings.'

I wanted to ask her whether dogs practised sex at that age, for I noticed him selecting a partner from among the other dogs in the park, with whom to exchange love and mate openly without embarrassment. I wanted to remark that a human being needed to be about twenty before discovering that babies did not drop from the sky. Instead I decided to benefit from the experience of the dog in tackling matters of love. I moved closer to her and put my arm around her shoulders and moved my head towards her to pluck a kiss from her lips, but Venus gently prevented me from reaching her mouth. She proceeded to relate amazing stories she had heard about the nature of dogs, their loyalty and intelligence until I begun to suspect that her line of work had something to do with dogs. I wanted to enquire about that but the blood that was playing a merry tune in me led me to tire of talking about them.

Confucius had by then got tangled up in a squabble with another dog over a female.

Venus leapt to her feet and rushed over, scolding him and telling him sharply to behave and stop fighting. I had begun to really dislike this dog whom I had invented in a moment of mischief, for he was now disturbing my happy mood and I felt clouds of resentment gathering in my breast.

Venus returned and sat down on the grass next to me, but my veins had stopped playing that happy tune. I could not understand what came over me in that instant but her face which appeared earlier so lovely and aristocratic, glowing with no make-up or artifice – the elegant dress with its print of suns and sea waves, her hair which looked as if five hand maidens had combined to dress it in an intricate style, arranged round her neck and head in a likeness only seen on the statues of Greek goddesses – all this appeared now as hollow as a descendant of love, artfully creating this illusion in order to practise her trade away from the meddling of the police. It wouldn't be long before she would name her price. I tried to dismiss this thought from my mind, for it was an injustice to this beautiful delicate lady who was intrigued by my playful ruse and had accompanied me to the park. Everything in her conduct and speech indicated that she was a lady from a high-class family, educated and cultured, a governor, an influential minister of status or a war hero. I was certain that her background was refined and distinguished.

But the evil thought had now taken control of my mind and spoilt my mood. It caused my feelings of pride at the skill with which I had contrived to talk to her, to evaporate into thin air.

So I resolved to take away the name I had given her and to dismiss her from the temple I had erected for her. I wanted to be the first to scare her off before she disillusioned me with the usual question of price.

'To be honest, I don't even like dogs ...'

She stopped talking. She sensed the hostility in my voice. There was no justification for terminating the game in such a tasteless and ungracious manner, but I went on :

'In fact, I hate them!'

She looked at me in astonishment as if wondering why I had allowed myself to invent such a dog for her, so full of vitality and energy. I no longer cared if my behaviour was disagreeable to such a high-born lady. What angered me most was that she was indeed from a high class.

'I went to a restaurant once which amused me a lot. They had grilled dog meat on the menu!'

I laughed gloatingly. I really did not know of any such restaurants which offered dog meat among their dishes. It was a lie I invented to spite her.

Confucius had gone away for some distance but now returned with another ball which he was pushing towards me. He ran around me excitedly to play, but met with no response. He instinctively sensed that I had begun to hate him. He immediately stopped playing and watched me apprehensively with ears cocked up in amazement. He whimpered unintelligibly as if expressing his shock

25

at the unpredictability which afflicts human behaviour.

I picked up the ball and threw it far back to its owners. I realised the game was now over, so I drew an imaginary gun from my pocket and aimed it at the dog's head. The woman screamed at me not to kill the dog. She pleaded and cried but I was not in the right state of mind to show any mercy either towards her or the dog. I viciously pulled the trigger and the sound of a shot rang through the air, scattering the birds who perched around the tree branches and filled the air with their terrified squawking. The other dogs playing in the park also ran in all directions. Confucius lay sprawled on the grass where he fell, bleeding and immobile. I left the woman standing there frozen in horror. I put my hands into my pockets and whistled merrily. When I looked up at the sky, there was the shape of a gigantic dog in the clouds above.

The dog eyed me in fury and pursued me with his barking as if he meant to harm me.

4

Radiant as the Sun

The place was a back street from which most of the buildings had turned their faces away, so that it became deserted, silent, devoid of life and movement. But as soon as the altercation broke out, the street was injected with a new spirit. A crowd of people suddenly burst forth from nowhere and came rushing to the place of the fight, milling around the protagonists. The air was filled with noise, clamour and violence. It was as if all those people had taken leave of their work and sat awaiting just such a happening, which when it did occur, they competed with each other in reaching the location and jostled each other in order to secure a vantage point up front from which to watch the spectacle at close range and enjoy a few moments of free entertainment.

I was returning to my car which I had parked in that back street. I had gone to the city shopping centre to buy some papers and magazines. With an involuntary movement, I raised my gaze over the heads of the crowd and realised that a violent confrontation was taking place between two men in the prime of their lives. Indeed they were mere teenagers, similar in appearance, both with long hair, wearing T-shirts and jeans. Despite the efforts of some of the spectators to separate them, their attempts only served to add more fuel to the young men's rage, increasing the tension and their determination to exchange blows and punches. Eventually those who intervened to stop the fight gave up and devoted themselves to watching and waiting to see who would kill the other one first.

I had satisfied my curiosity and stopped watching. I proceeded to where I had parked my car, but a mysterious shiver took possession of my whole body. I was aware that I had seen the shadow of a woman on the scene, who most probably was the cause of the fight. She appeared embarrassed, humiliated, unsuccessfully trying to sink her head between her shoulders as if trying to hide it inside her body. I suddenly stood rooted to the spot, overwhelmed by an inexplicable feeling that I knew this woman. I only required a swift glance to recognise immediately that this woman standing near the fighting men was no other than Leila. The sudden discovery confused me. What devil had cast her here amidst this crowd and made her party to this awful fight? I threw the bundle of papers to the ground and rushed in a storm of demented fury towards the men. I grasped the girl by her shoulders with all my strength and shook her, demanding an explanation for what was going on, the reason for her presence and her connection with these two sparring bulls.

Leila burst out crying, unable to speak. I told her to go on home immediately and I would follow her later for an explanation. I then turned on the two men with all my anger and passion and started to throw indiscriminate punches to the left and to the right, receiving them in turn but not feeling anything. I heard a few words of praise from some of the spectators at the way I stormed the battle, which increased my determination to carry this out to the end. I wasn't aware of how much time elapsed, but when eventually a policeman arrived on the scene and took us all to the station, I was exhausted, worn out, hardly able to walk. I felt sticky blood running down my forehead. My mind was befuddled, hardly able to grasp what had happened, except for a blurred image of an empty street suddenly filling with people, papers strewn all over the ground, a fight taking place between two men I didn't know, and Leila appearing on the scene for a yet unknown reason.

There was nothing for me to say, when my turn came for the policeman to question me, but to tell him the truth. I saw two men quarrelling over my fiancée, so I had no alternative but to fight them off.

'So she's your fiancée?'

'She was my fiancée.'

I found myself saying this without any previous justification. I still did not know the reason for the fight, nor why Leila was present in that place. There was something suspicious about the circumstances, but soon all would be revealed. This incident undoubtedly touched upon both my honour and pride, and I was called upon to terminate the relationship which bound me to this woman for over two years and which culminated in announcing our engagement three months ago.

I remembered my mother and her joy when I informed her that I had at last found the woman I'd been searching for. My mother had spent several years roaming the houses of relatives and neighbours looking for a respectable girl, as a wife for me. As soon as I refused one of her offers, she came up with another one regarding another girl who was better educated, richer or more beautiful. I used to try and rebuff her persistence by explaining to her that the woman who was to share my life must be chosen by me alone and not by my mother. I must get to know her first and find out whether I could love her or not, and that I was unwilling to submit to the traditional way, even if I remained a bachelor till the end of time. It was a custom which was cruel to both the man and the woman, the latter led cattle-like to the house of a man she had never seen or known before. I tried to explain all this to her to no avail, for she continued her search, bringing me now and then fresh news of yet another girl she had seen who looked as 'radiant as the sun', but she met with no agreement from me. Eventually she despaired and ceased her attempts for a few years, leaving her fate up to the will of God. It was as if she sensed that I was weary of the subject so she never broached it to me again.

Three months ago I presented her with Leila, asking her opinion about this girl becoming my wife and her daughter. My mother filled the air with her cries of joy, her wrinkled face lit up, her illness and pallor left her. I thought of her and also of Leila and the letters she wrote me.

They were restrained, bashful, as if she regarded disclosing her feelings a crime or a sin. Yet she said more in her coy words than was expressed in frank letters. 'I read your letter and memorised its contents by heart', was the most she allowed by way of confession, which in its simplicity delighted me and filled me with happiness.

I remembered the pleasure of leaving home early on cold winter mornings, after we had firmly established our relationship, to give her a lift in my car to school. I deliberately arrived an hour or so before classes started so I could have the opportunity of strolling and talking with her in the streets of the city. I remembered all this, also the songs which she made me like. I didn't care much in the past for following the latest trends in music, but we grew to derive great pleasure from listening to them together; just as I got her to appreciate poetry as much as I did. I introduced her to all the classical poets whom I admired, and she grew to like them even more than I did. We vied with each other in discovering a poem, or a song, which better expressed the strength and depth of our love. All this talk now seemed ridiculous, like scenes from a comic play. This matter has now ended in this event, these blows which I felt all over my face, the clammy thread of blood which trickled down my forehead, and the statement which I found myself saying with no will of my own:

'She was my fiancée.'

She wasn't just my fiancée, she was the only beautiful wondrous thing in my life. The bleakness of the relationships around me, the dimness of our social life and its wretchedness, the limited opportunities for establishing human relationships between the men and women of our society, made me feel that my life was a mere exhausting journey in the desert, causing it to drag heavily, sluggishly, empty and meaningless until the arrival of Leila and her love which descended like a city from heaven, transforming the shape of the desert all around me. I had arrived at a stage in my life when I despaired of ever establishing any relationship with any girl in our society. I didn't know how things would turn out for me as I felt my youth slip between my fingers. Here I was already in my thirties, which would soon hand me over to my forties, which I perceived as the 'wolf' waiting to devour what hope remained for me. Yet I refused to give way to my mother's exhortations to throw myself submissively and willingly into the well of traditions. I preferred the 'wolf' to the 'pit'. I used to reflect, as my hair started to thin, that the wolf was approaching but I struggled against this. I resisted reaching forty with all my strength even had I been routed, I refused to submit. There were many men who loved and married when they were over fifty or even over sixty. That's what I convinced myself with, but it was only mere talk for amusement and consolation; for I did indeed feel vanquished and that I was embarked on an already losing battle and the journey was exhausting me. Despair crept into my heart and I had to admit defeat ...

Suddenly Leila's face shone through and I began to experience the warmth of this kind of human relationship. I discovered that her family had adopted the spirit of the modern age, and permitted a relationship between their daughter and myself to develop out in the light and fresh air. I realised that good fortune had led me to her, or placed her in my path, whereas other younger men who were more handsome and richer than myself, and who had a more modern outlook on life, still could not find such an opportunity and they jumped one after the other into that well and resigned themselves to a traditional way of marriage. Leila became my life. Nothing occupied my mind but her and I only looked forward to my meetings with her. I existed in the hope of the day when we would be joined together in wedded bliss.

Everything was ruined now and once more I was lost on my own in the desert, that city had now disappeared for it was nothing but a mirage. Let the police do what they must, I was innocent and my crime was her doing. It was in the policeman's power to close the file if he so wished and allow me to go on my way, for I no longer had any connection with this matter. I would then go straight to

Antonio's bar and, with the aid of a drink or two, regain some of my wits which had deserted me. Also to find a little consolation with either Franca or Janet. Then I remembered that Antonio and his prostitutes had left the country for good. The selling of alcohol was banned and the only thing left for me as a means of escape was my car. I decided to drive aimlessly through the streets of the city until I regained my composure and equilibrium.

I handed the car over to what I called the 'automatic driver', that part of my unconscious brain which drove the car automatically without any conscious effort on my part. I was thus free to reflect upon what had happened, for some aspects were still vague. All I heard at the police station was that one of the men involved in the fight had seen the other one annoying the girl, so he took it upon himself to defend her although she was a complete stranger. I could not bring myself to believe this fabricated story, for there was more to it than met the eye. The men were fighting as if they bore each other a grudge lasting a hundred years. Or as if the contest was over a treasure which would make the winner the richest man in the world. This story was but a clever ruse to escape the consequences which would arise had one of them confessed the true reason. The whole matter involved defamation of character and honour which would lead to complications such as courts, legal action and even prison. They were much too clever to fall into that trap. I congratulated them inwardly at their brightness in inventing that story. No doubt they were from a younger generation which was more intelligent and devious. Their development had been unfolding in a freer society from the one I was brought up in. They were the result of mixed primary schools, so they were more forward with the opposite sex, more daring in taking the initiative.

Perhaps one of them shared the same school bench with Leila and had formed an association with her. The cause of the fight puzzled me but I didn't wish to know it in case the latter was true. What it boiled down to was that her conduct astonished me. I could not fathom the reasons for her running away from one relationship straight into the next, and in such a manner that it would injure my esteem. True there was some gap in our ages, but this couldn't be held responsible for her sudden change of heart. She had loved me for myself, there was no other compulsion such as money, or prestige, or being related to her which might have influenced her to love me and agree to be my future life partner. Had she been deceiving me all that while? That question would remain a mystery. I wasn't so old-fashioned as to forbid the woman to whom I was betrothed from going out into the streets unveiled, or to go shopping or to meet people. On the contrary, I had no objection to her travelling on her own or going to restaurants or the theatre or parties without me. All these activities were above reproach as long as the woman herself is above reproach, as Othello said in Shakespeare's play. It was another matter finding her in a compromising situation, involved with two men fighting over her, or laying bets as to which victor would win this prize – my fiancée – in a duel carried out without gloves, swords or the presence of seconds. Undoubtedly my reputation and upbringing could not tolerate such a thing.

I found myself being driven by that automatic driver, with no intervention on my part, and stopping by a deserted spot on the beach which I used to frequent with Leila whenever possible to steal some fleeting moments from time. So here was the sea. I stopped the engine and got out to stand awhile in the company of this great friend. I was met by the odour of the sea and I filled my lungs with it. I listened to its waves conversing in a tumultuous and roaring language to the rocks on the shore. I found a parallel between the tempo of the sea and the emotions and reactions that were surging in my breast. This brought me some comfort and cleared my mind. I began to review the situation in a less emotional way and things appeared much easier than they did at first. I realised that in the presence of this sea which stretched endlessly that most problems were usually trivial and insignificant, but we transformed them with our emotions into something awful and as huge as mountains. I wasn't at that moment making a comparison between what had taken place and the expanse of this sea or the enormity of the universe, only measuring it by the general unimportant events which usually occur in our lives.

I had not actually caught Leila in the arms of one of her lovers, or in his bed, to get worked up to such a state. She was most probably crossing the road and if a fight arose over her, why should she bear the blame? I found myself laughing at the way I stormed the fight, when the only normal thing for me to do was take Leila by the hand and lead her back home. I had not met one witness so far who contradicted the story I heard at the police station. I began to recall that on a day-to-day basis throughout our relationship, I had not perceived any situation, word, deed or even a faint whisper emanating from her which could justify my suspicious thoughts. So where on earth did this new friendship I had imagined spring from? The whole incident was unpremeditated. It happened as she was on her way to buy a pencil, or a copy book, or a book. I found myself greatly relieved at this conclusion which my majestic friend the sea had led me to. I was doing an injustice to this innocent young woman who had granted me her love. For the first time I thought of her love as a gift from God, presented only to the pure at heart amongst His worshippers. How dared I reject this offering, this beautiful gift which gave my life new meaning unlike the lives of millions of other people who did not possess such a love. A love to rid their lives of savage loneliness which devoured their days and sentenced them to spiritual exile. How could I be so ungrateful as to reject this blessing?

I looked at my watch and realised that the night was still young. No doubt Leila had returned home and was siting there all that while crying, and awaiting my arrival. So I must now offer my thanks and gratitude to this sea, and go to her immediately to inform her that I would never cease to love her or allow anything in the world to disturb the calm of her life. I would seek out the youth who annoyed her and punish him severely.

My beloved opened the door, reproaching me for being late for my appointed visit, and asking me about the women's magazine I promised to bring her. I said nothing until we had entered and were seated. She was surprised at the wound on my forehead and the traces of blood on my shirt. My girl was dismayed as she asked me what had happened, as if she had no part in the incident – if not the sole cause of it! I thought to myself that perhaps she wished to conceal the incident from her mother, who no sooner was in the sitting room than she left it. I waited till her mother had gone, then asked her to forget the whole affair and pretend that nothing had happened. She still didn't know what I was talking about, so I explained that I was very upset to start with but now that I knew the true reason for the squabble, I saw no reason why we should discuss the matter further. It was merely a passing episode and best laughed off. As for that worthless young man who annoyed her, he probably had received enough beating to leave him with a permanent injury! Yet everything was still a mystery to her and she kept asking me, although we were alone in the room, about what incident I was talking about, what fight and what young man because she had not left the house that evening, had not set foot in that street all day, had not witnessed a fight, had not met a young man or woman and had not seen me since I gave her a lift home from school!

What had happened to this girl's brains?! I repeated the story, recounting every minute detail, but she still insisted that the girl I had seen was without doubt someone else. She knew nothing about the matter. How could she expect me to believe this? If I had just glimpsed her from a distance I could have reasoned that another woman who resembled her made me think it was Leila, but I had stood close beside her, my face close to hers, talking to her. I had held her by the shoulders as she cried. I had asked her to return home and she complied and went away. I hysterically refused to accept the fact that the girl I had seen was someone else, so she called her mother in as a witness. She swore that her daughter had never left the house, not even for a moment since returning home from school. I told Leila perhaps this was a trick to extricate herself from a situation not of her doing, but that I considered the subject a trivial passing incident which would not affect our love or our engagement, so why couldn't she confess the truth and be done with it? I was getting really agitated and angry. How could I have made a mistake in recognising Leila? How could I not tell the difference between her and another woman unless I was suffering from some kind of hallucination or mania? Was the fight just fanciful imagination? Was the street and the crowd just a nightmare? But the wound was still present on my forehead and the bloodstains still on my shirt. The investigating police officer with the blemish on the side of his nose was no spectre. Everything did actually happen! Eventually I left the house in a temper, slamming the front door violently behind me and leaving Leila crying with her head on her mother's lap.

Who was this other woman who had borrowed Leila's features, her height, her hair, who wore her clothes and stood in my path and started the fight around her, in which I became involved? I loved Leila – this fact alone was sufficient to convince me from the start that it was not her, but another girl who resembled her. But she didn't just look like her, it was her and no one else! I was convinced of this as I was of my own name and of the occurrence of the fight and the mark left on my forehead; as convinced as I was of what took place in that street, in that location, and in that hour!

In the following days when I returned to take Leila to school as usual, I didn't experience any joy. What motivated me was not a longing to see her, but a compulsion to throw some light on this darkness which filled my mind. I kept insisting that she sharpen her memory afresh because I had read of some instances where a person suppresses his memory temporarily, because his conscious brain refuses to face the facts – if the latter are a cause of great distress and anguish. Leila only laughed at this theory and asked me to forget the whole thing. She was even prepared to retract her words

34

and pretend to confess what I wanted to hear if this would solve the problem. However, my problem had no solution. I was unable to relinquish for one moment my utter conviction that the girl I had seen was none other than Leila. In spite of my resolution to put the whole incident behind me, and to cease thinking or worrying about it, I felt it infiltrating the love which joined me to Leila and throwing a heavy shadow over it. Our meetings lacked the previous delight and radiance they once had, our laughter no longer had that spontaneous and happy innocent ring about it. I contrived my own laughter so she would not suspect that my feelings towards her had changed. I still loved her, but my love was wretched and gloomy. A strange tiredness pervaded my soul and made it heavy with an inexplicable worry. It was not mistrust in her conduct or doubting my ability to love her, but something else which didn't take long before I found an explanation for.

One evening I saw a woman who looked like Leila enter a restaurant, accompanied by another woman and two men I didn't know. To confirm my doubt, I followed them and approached the table which the waiter had led them to. I discovered that it indeed was Leila. Everything was made clear in the brilliant lights of the restaurant. She was laughing shamelessly and was wearing a low cut and revealing dress. Her hair style was different, like that of a film star. Her face was covered with heavy make-up. What was this strange transformation in her conduct and appearance? I felt sick but I controlled myself as I rushed towards the table and greeted her in order to surprise her. My presence, however, was no great shock. She did not cry out or faint as I had expected. She looked at me without interest. I did not want to cause a scandal in the restaurant, so I bent towards her and whispered between clenched teeth, struggling to overcome the feeling of nausea:

'What are you doing here, you ...'

I didn't actually say the word 'bitch' but left it hanging in the air. She looked at me in amazement but without recognition, as if I had been a ghost just risen from the grave to spoil people's enjoyment of life.

'Who are you?'

How could she be so brazen?! I had enough venom in me to blow up the restaurant with all it contained of customers, waiters, tables and fare, but I exercised the utmost of control in checking my temper, as well as any other person faced with the same situation. I told her that contrary to what she might think, I was not angry or miserable, just glad that at last the truth was revealed after years of lies and deception.

'You must be crazy!'

Yes, yes, that's exactly what you have been aiming for all along when you denied your presence in that street the moment the fight broke out between two of your lovers. Each one wanting to claim you exclusively for himself, each loath to see the other share your body, so they fought. Then your mother colluded with you and covered up for you until you both made me doubt what I did, saw and heard.

I was the victim of a gang I mistook for a family able to absorb the spirit of the modern age, but they were setting traps for me – what spirit is this and what age is this?!

One of the waiters was trying to calm down the man sitting next to the woman and prevent him from attacking me. He got hold of my hand and forcibly pulled me towards the door, threatening to call the police if I annoyed the customers further. The shock was greater than the waiter or his threat. The thing which stunned me most, more than her betrayal, and filled my heart with dread, was discovering that Leila, who normally had such a shy demure nature, so much so that she didn't even lift her gaze off the ground, was now revealing an outrageous nature, shameless and wanton. Was my judgement so impaired?

An idea suddenly occurred to me and I planned to carry it out immediately. I would drive over as fast as a maniac to Leila's house. I shouldn't give her mother a chance to deny that her daughter had ever left the house that evening. I would force her to accompany me to the restaurant to see for herself what her daughter was doing. I should also fetch her father and her brothers and all the relatives I could find. I would make them all witnesses to her betrayal. If they refused to accompany me then this would mean that they were all accomplices in a secret web of vice and I would expose them to the whole world!

I jumped into my car and drove like a madman. I banged at the door violently. My astonishment knew no bounds when Leila herself opened the door with no make-up, no strange hairdo, no daring evening gown. I raised my head up to the sky and implored help from the immense universe, the stars which filled the sky, the known and unknown creatures of the dark, the angels and the devils, for I could not comprehend anything that was happening now. How could Leila have managed to borrow a rocket in a few minutes and return home, wash off all the make-up, change the hairstyle, take off the evening gown and put on a simple house dress?! I breathlessly

36

demanded :

'Were you outside the house just now?'

The question was stupid and I didn't expect an answer. She herself did not reply. She just laughed sarcastically and pointed to her dress and appearance. I realised finally that I had been indeed paranoiac and it was only now that I was willing to believe that she was telling the truth all along when she said that the woman at the scene of the fight was someone else; as was the case with this other woman I saw sitting next to her husband or boyfriend this evening.

Thereafter, I continued to see Leila a lot – in different places and different situations: frequenting restaurants or going to cinemas, strolling in shops with one companion, or going for a car trip with another; wearing the uniform of an air hostess or a tourist booking a room at a hotel. I stopped going up to her angrily and starting a quarrel from which I would retreat wounded. I found myself compelled in the beginning to approach each woman I imagined was Leila, but soon remembered it wasn't her but that an obsession had taken control of my mind and was forcing me to see her embodied in all these women. I realised that if I carried on like this I would spend the rest of my days in a mental institution. This thought frightened me and prevented me from sleep. I stayed awake for two or three days, dozing off fitfully for a few hours then lying awake once more. I didn't consult a doctor or a psychiatrist. I was scared. I knew that an illness like this would only cease with the termination of my association with Leila. It was a hard choice - as difficult as a person amputating his own leg, hand or arm.

When I informed my mother that I had broken off my engagement to Leila, she didn't seem surprised. It was as if for a mysterious reason she was expecting something like this to happen. Or as if she had already resigned herself to spending the rest of her life without seeing me with a home of my own, a wife or children. To snap her out of her despair, I finally said :

'You told me about five years ago that one of the neighbours had a daughter who was as "radiant as the sun" and, ...'

She didn't allow me to finish my sentence. She immediately put on her veil and coat and left the house. No doubt that 'daughter of the sun' was married by now with five children, perhaps has had twins, and ended up with ten children! Yet, somewhere close by our house another neighbour may have an unmarried daughter who was also 'as radiant as the sun'. My mother with her judgement and experience of life, might decide that this girl would make me a suitable wife. My mother, who had left the house before I'd finished speaking, was probably even now initiating the engagement formalities with the girl's family. I would leave everything up to her and she would bring me my 'sun'; but for the time being I went to bed for some sleep.

5

The Last Station

No sooner had I opened the door and saw her sitting near the window – as a waft of her perfume hit me in the face – than my head was filled with the strains of some demented feverish music, performed by a band whose musicians excelled in beating the drums with their heads and the heels of their shoes, and a guitarist who almost bit the strings and strummed them with his teeth, and howled his song. I stood at the door for an instant to regain my breath and remove the strain from my arm after carrying my suitcase. The woman raised her eyes towards me and in a corner of my memory night club lights flashed, the sort which blinked on and off in the fashion of fire engines, ambulances and police cars; and where the dancers underneath those lights gyrated hysterically as if worshipping god of violence, sex and crime.

I asked her permission to sit down and she nodded her head. In my mind there stirred images from spy thriller reels, scenes which alternated from police chases to torrid love adventures. Something about this woman exuded stimulation, seduction and sex appeal. She sat quietly in her seat, attentively reading a large book spread over her knees, and wearing eye glasses, for she had probably strained her eyesight in too much studying and reading.

She wore a grey jacket and had folded a long scarf several times round her neck. It appeared that she had made a fine art out of camouflage on this autumn day which had borrowed something from winter days. Yet in spite of all this protection she had the kind of beauty which would still proclaim itself no matter how well hidden. Hers was an aggressive beauty, like a tiger which is unleashed to devour you as soon as you approach; but it became apparent to me that she was greatly embarrassed by this beauty, with its violent, ferocious and torrid quality.

She wore her glasses and all those clothes and placed the largest books possible on her lap in a desperate effort to stem the rebelliousness of that unruly beauty. She even declined from wearing even a hint of lipstick or emollient so that her lips appeared parched and dry. She had bound her well-endowed and thrusting breasts within the most sedate and severe clothes, imprisoning them

39

so cruelly. She chose the dullest shade of grey and bought a scarf at least a hundred feet long to rap round her neck to prevent even a glimmer of smooth marble-like neck from peeping out or twinkling through. As for those eyes with the thick long lashes which sent out flashes like the guns used by aliens from the other planets in science fiction films, with the power to smite and destroy, she had tried to remedy the situation by wearing her glasses, which she now uses for reading. One can sense from the first instant that she took great pains to conceal her beauty or at least to subdue and submerge it; for no doubt it had caused her a great deal of annoyance at every stage of her life. She had not been able to live anywhere without fights breaking out amongst the young men in the neighbourhood because of her. She had not been able to go out into the street without attracting a crowd, which in turn drew the attention of the keepers of law and order. She had not been able to enter a restaurant, or a place of public entertainment, or a shop or business premises without people neglecting their business to stare at her. Perhaps she had grown accustomed to this reaction and had reached a high standard of controlling her beauty, and taming its wildness. That's how she was able to walk down the street, and enter a restaurant or a place of entertainment and avoid all these demonstrations and rivalry. She had succeeded in keeping the tigers within her safely locked away in their cages and that's why she now sat calmly in her seat, unaware that those tigers only needed a tourist from an Eastern country like me, with a longing for life, to cause them to bound out of their cages, smashing their chains and breaking the locks to sink their claws and teeth into his flesh.

The thick fog outside was pressing like a pack of hyenas a few metres away from the station. I had sprawled on the opposite seat next to the door and wished I had the courage to sit next to her or directly opposite. This would facilitate the opportunity of striking up a conversation with her, but what could I do to change a shy nature that had been my lot all my life? It was brave enough of me to sit in a compartment alone with her at all, and not run away because of embarrassment, which her beauty was arousing in me. I thanked God that the train had moved before other passengers had the chance to occupy the seats which separated us. I didn't have the time to buy a newspaper or a magazine with which to occupy myself during the journey. I barely managed to catch the train at the last minute. She was content to read her book and had no need to turn to something else to pass the time, such as entering into a casual conversation with an unknown companion on the journey. She didn't lift her head off the book, for she had used it as a barricade to discourage any intruders from approaching the gardens of her palace.

I started to invent reasons to justify my failure to strike up a conversation with her. I pretended that I would have succeeded with this woman if only I could have met her on her own without that accursed book. I watched the trees flashing past, and the fields which stretched far into the distance, shrouded in the morning mist and managed to pass the time by reading the book of nature. I started to invest the shapes outside covered by the mist with other meanings, imagining that some were tents, while others looked like riders wearing white-clothes, mounting white horses and stirring up clouds of dust around them, but suddenly nature disappeared.

The train entered a tunnel and I noticed that inside the compartment pale yellow lights became visible in the gloom. Their effect transformed the woman into what painters must have imagined the Virgin Mary to look like. I saw her suddenly acquire a saintly glow which endowed her with a calm strange beauty. She appeared as if she did not belong to this world. She was a saint reading her bible and intoning her prayers in a deserted temple high up on a mountain top, kneeling there at dawn and worshipping alone in the lamplight.

We emerged from the tunnel and the holy mantle slipped off. Once more the rowdy music started to flow from her breasts, her lips and her eyes. The reels of sex and violence once again emerged from the blonde hair cascading over her shoulders; the car chases and the fire engine flowed from the pages of the book spread over her knees. I instantly pictured her with various lovers and presumed that she was on her way back from visiting the one in the country, who had bought her a mansion there. She was now going to her lover who lived in the city. He had moved to live in with her after divorcing his wife and abandoning his children and quitting his job. She would then kick him out after squandering all his money.

There was also the student whom she had enticed away from his studies and who now made ends meet hanging round bars and night spots. The fourth, fifth or sixth who had spent all his money on her, even to the extent of selling his business and closing up shop or firm, had gone bankrupt.

The seventh or eighth had lost his job or his mind. She also had relationships with some politicians, in the event of one of them becoming a minister of state; but a rival for this lovely lady's affections was the chief editor of a national newspaper who had discovered a scandal concerning the minister and had exposed him.

41

This had caused a sensation in political circles which led to the downfall of the government and the current party in power was out of favour, having lost the confidence of the nation. She had now got rid of all her previous lovers and kept only one. I imagined him to be, in order to control her seductive powers, a very tough and cruel man with a powerful build. I chose for him a violent profession. In spite of losing the sight of one eye, he was the second-in-command of a large gang engaged in smuggling and drugs. I wanted him to be the second in command of the organisation because he would have to be the man of action, entrusted with the job of carrying things out. The top man always planned and organised. I didn't want him to be the brains, but merely the steel arm manipulated by the brains. I didn't mind reserving a place for him near the top of the ladder of success to which he aspired. His ambition would reveal other ugly aspects of his nature when a rival gang would use him to plot the elimination of his boss who was his benefactor and who had helped him and promoted him to his present position in the organisation.

I mused to myself that it was a great shame that she got herself involved in a relationship with the one-eyed man. Suffice it the wide age gap between them – for in spite of his powerfully large frame and a health as strong as an ox – he was approaching 50 while she was merely 21 or 22. I wished he could have valued that beauty, but even if he did appreciate it, he only persisted in vanquishing and humiliating it. He saw himself as an opponent in a battle in which his ugliness and uncouthness (his face was full of warts and he had a flat shaped bald head), would triumph over the charms of this woman, her allure and her bewitching beauty which shone from her eyes, her hair, her neck, her brow, her breasts and her lips. He realised that should he weaken, his defeat would be assured and he would lose that enchanting female forever. He had triumphed over her because from the very beginning he had treated her with viciousness, as if avenging all the ugly faces in the world against this woman who was the symbol of beauty, and who suffered on behalf of all the beautiful creatures on the face of this earth. He had discovered in treating her thus a new aspect to his personality, an agreeable and pleasing feeling, and he derived pleasure from hurting and humiliating her.

Whenever he desired her, he savagely tore the clothes off her, ripping them with his nails, piece by piece, until she was completely naked. I had guessed from his coarse features that he was not merely content with hitting her with his hands or kicking her with his feet, but that he used chairs, dishes, pieces of furniture and even kitchen utensils against her as a punishment, whenever she raised her voice at him. Despite her present demeanour which conveyed a regal dignity, I knew how she suffered and screamed as she knelt at his feet, weeping and begging for mercy and pity. This only increased his violence and his desire to humiliate and torment her. Afterwards he took her almost by force. I noticed a small scratch on her left temple which confirmed all my suspicions. I was certain that his fingernails had left their mark on her face. She was obviously trying to cover the traces beneath her hair and was using the heavy scarf to conceal the bruises which her neck had sustained as a result of his sadistic treatment.

The image of horses conjured up by the fog dissipated as the morning sun bathed the green fields which stretched as far as the horizon. The world appeared beautiful and cheerful. I realised that I was falling irresistibly in love with this woman whose delicious mouth burst with forbidden desires. She lifted her head off the pages of the book and her eyes swept across the floor of the compartment and came to rest on my face for a few seconds, as if she had just discovered my presence. I felt a tremor run through me, as if I had crept stealthily into a queen's bedchamber, who would then call the guards and have me killed. I dropped my gaze to the floor so our eyes would not meet, for fear that she might discover the thoughts which ran in my mind. She returned to her book, after she had excused and forgiven me. I felt remorseful for filling her life with all that terror and for having firmly secured its chains around her, like the three lower circles in Dante's hell. I thanked God that our thoughts had no voice, otherwise she would have screamed for help after discovering what I had been secretly thinking about her. If I was brave I could have approached her with a pleasant remark about the beauty of the morning. The shyness which had been my companion all my life prevented me from making the first move. I made a resolution that I would stop myself falling in love with all women, until I could find an exceptionally attractive woman who would strike up a conversation with me first! I would devote all my love to her! Still I remembered that there was an ogre in the life of this female, who laid siege around her and prevented her from addressing strangers. The shadow of the ugly man followed her everywhere she went. He watched all her looks, her words and her movements. I was certain that he had her followed and that someone was spying on us this very minute through a chink in the door. The poor wretch could not escape his clutches, for he had threatened her with death should she even contemplate leaving him. Yet there must be a way of saving her. Why didn't she leave him and escape to a distant country and put an end to this existence, filled with violence and misery? There was the problem of where she could find the money to enable her to afford the costs of the journey and settling down somewhere. She was of humble origins and her family were so poor they were reduced to begging. Her mother could not afford any medications and had died from a fever. Her father was taken to an old people's home. Her aunt lived in the country and that awful man did not allow her to visit except once or twice a year. The aunt lived alone and depended on some aid from her niece. She was probably back on her way from a short visit now. She had saved every extra penny she had to help out her aunt. What a noble character!

I was filled with pain, thinking of a way to save her from all this misery. I watched her as she read her book, exuding her magic in dignity and silence. My love for her increased and I wished that she was indeed a queen and I was her secret lover, visiting her furtively and enfolding her royal body tenderly. That body which was like a richly laded table, brimming with delicacies, strolling across its gardens filled with blooms, then ascending to its high balconies, picking what I fancied from its abundance of apples, grapes or pomegranates, and drinking from its mature vintage wines. In the midst of my ecstasy at possessing this body through whose veins blue blood ran, a thought struck me. Why didn't she inform the police about him?!

That was her only way out to free herself from his clutches and end her years of misery, spent in his company. He would be thrown behind bars and would not be released from a gloomy prison until he was a very old man.

Don't worry about what would happen to you afterwards. I shall hasten to your side. I shall labour and suffer to make you happy. Oh delight of my heart, I shall be your obedient servant worshipping at your altar. I shall help your beauty regain its respect and shall offer you such love as no man has given a woman before me. I had been looking at her, glad that the time was approaching to save her, but for some reason, I saw her throw the book she held between her hands to the floor. She leapt up, anger consuming her brow and her face darkened with a strange sorrow as if she had seen the most horrible and awful vision. She rapidly advanced towards me. I rose from my seat and looked at her with astonishment. I saw her hand rise and I felt the sting of a violent slap across my face, as if I had committed the most heinous crime against her!

'You scoundrel!'

I was so taken aback, I didn't know what to do and remained standing there speechless. I hadn't been sitting close enough so that any movement on my part could have justified a mistaken interpretation. I tried to say something but I heard her shouting at me, tears stinging her eyes:

'What business is it of you to entertain such sick thoughts about saving me? Who gave you the right to interfere in my affairs or act on my behalf? It's my life and I am free to do whatever I like with it.'

I remained transfixed in my spot, overwhelmed with confusion and shock. I was transformed into a statue made of clay or wood, unable to comprehend or act or reason or see or hear or speak. I didn't know how much time elapsed while in this state. When life began to return to my wooden frame I felt the floor of the compartment shudder underneath my feet. I realised the train had put on its brakes and it reached the last station. A porter opened the door of the carriage and asked us to get ready to leave the train. He saw me standing there looking bewildered and saw her sitting there crying. He looked at me curiously and asked her what had happened, but she didn't reply. She collected her bags and hastily departed. The porter thought I was her companion and said with a smile :

'Don't worry about it! Tiffs will happen between lovers!'

I saw him standing there on the platform through the window. He was an immense giant of about fifty. His head was flat shaped and bald. His face was full of warts. One eye was covered by a patch, the other eye as expectantly looking at those descending the train.

6

A Man from Ireland

You have come at the right time. This friend of yours is really interesting. My name is Frank. Frank O'Brien. From Ireland. May I order you a drink? This will give me an excuse to speak to this 'princess', the waitress of the pub. I have something to tell her. Ha ha ha! Do not let my appearance fool you my friend. I am still young. I could tell he was a stranger, so I came to talk to him. These cities are cruel to strangers. I experienced that when I came over from Dublin to this city for the first time. You would not find anybody talking to you. It's as if every one of them is keeping a big secret to himself, and fears that if he indulged in conversation with strangers his secret will unfold, and a great punishment would befall him. His English is not fluent, but I understand from him that he is going to Ireland on a training course. I was pleased to know that Ireland was a place to go to, to study. Tell him that. Also, tell him that I thought that men at his age did not take much interest in going to school and attending courses, therefore I admire him for being so ambitious. He is going to Scotland, then. Ah! I misunderstood him. But it does not matter. Tell him also that he should not worry too much about the language problem. In Ireland they will respect you more if you don't speak good English. What a big surprise it will be to them! They think that everyone has forgotten his original language, and speaks only English. They feel guilty because they forgot their original language and gave themselves up to this foreign tongue. You will learn quickly and you will find yourself talking to them as if you were one of them. Ireland is very different from England. Dublin is not London. You will be surrounded by many friends. People will come over to you just to talk, as I am doing now. They have no secrets torturing them; secrets about which they are worried, in case they leak to strangers. Tell him that. Excuse me for a minute. I only want to ask her when she's coming. She promised to meet me last Sunday. She has given me nine or ten dates, but has never turned up. Maybe she is ridiculing me. But I am sure that some day she will lose her senses and keep her date. I'm sure that once, when the hour of our meeting approaches, she will find herself lonely at home, fed up and full of emptiness, not knowing what to do with herself, and instead of staying there on her own contemplating death or suicide she will take her handbag and come out to meet me. He is going to Scotland then. Tell him that people in Ireland do not trust anybody unless he is very good at telling lies and crafty in making them up. Did you tell him that? They love nothing more than a man who knows how to tell stories about his imaginary glories. They love hearing lies more than any other people in the world. They will admire you more once they know that you are a good liar. He is a welder, then, sent by the Ports Authority, on a training course to Scotland, but is better to describe himself as a writer. In Ireland they think of a writer as something of a Saint, and instead of talking about ports, welding, and ironsmiths, he should talk to them, from the moment he arrives there, about poems inspired by Ireland that he dreams of writing, and the novel which he is writing under contract for an international film company, but cannot find enough enthusiasm to finish it. His creative bent hates commitments, agreements and contracts. These are things which are in conflict with his free nature. He may tell them that in any language and they will understand. They will think highly of him. They love God; and they drink alcohol till death. They take their children to church on Sundays, and love listening to lies. They are honest with themselves, therefore you have to be truthful in telling these white lies about yourself. It is not necessary to claim that one of your friends is a minister or your father was the Secretary General of the United Nations, or that one of your ancestors was a king or a leader. These things will not make you seem any better. Tell him that. There is a certain romance in their nature which loves adventure, for instance, the one day you went on a tiger hunting trip, in a forest. This story will make them look upon you as a hero whom everybody will be honoured to meet, or to buy a drink, or to take home for dinner. It does not matter if you were heart broken, for instance, you had a sweetheart who could not find a way to reach you for one reason or another. These are many as far as I know, in the countries of the East. Maybe she took her life by taking a whole bottle of sleeping pills, and you are grieving for her. You left your city, running away from her memories. You will find them, crying with you, real tears. They will be doing the best to console and comfort you. Tell him that. Tell him that they, in Ireland, prefer this kind of suicide where death comes to man while he is unconscious. That is why they are addicted to drink. They become more addicted the closer they get to death. So death does not befall them suddenly, while they are sober or awake. He is going to Scotland then. Sometimes I do forget this. But tell him you will love the Irish more. You will find that they will love you if you know how to make their good hearts happy with white lies of no harm to anyone. He can even tell them that he had met Picasso before he died, and that he had drink with Ezra Pound on his last days, and that he keeps some correspondence with one of the big stars of the theatre, a singer, or a musician. These things cost nothing and harm nobody, but will make them love him much. Women are more vulnerable when they hear the name of the theatre and popstars. Tell him that. I see on his finger an engagement ring or wedding ring. Now in fact I didn't know what it means to have the ring on your left hand. It's been a long time since that experience, from which I learned that I was not made to be a husband. I advise anyone going to Dublin to take this ring off. Women will run away from his company not only because of the Catholic values which are still a motive and mover of relationships with women. Tell him that. I see him smiling. I know of this longing for women which fills the hearts of men from the East. My father in his moment of anger used to belittle my mother for being of gypsy origins. Now I'm proud of this hot gypsy blood in my veins. I can't see anything in life more joyful, noble, or glorious than looking into the eyes of a beautiful woman ha.. ha.. ha.. I don't just look, I usually go beyond that. If you want to benefit from my advice you will find someone to buy you a drink in a pub, throw you a party, and invite the most beautiful girls for you if you knew how to take on the appearance of a poet misunderstood by the world. Ireland then will come to you, with dignity and pride to prove to you that it is the only place in the world which can understand and shelter poets of your kind. Tell him that. I'm sorry, sometimes I forget to give you enough time to translate what I say. You speak good English. You must have been in this city for long. You must know something about the difference between the nature of the English and the Irish. Most of the guests in this pub are from Ireland. Yes, the publican is from Dublin. He's an old friend. We both emigrated from there. I love Ireland, but where I find enough money to live in comfort becomes my home. Dublin is a great city. Tell him that. I am happy to see someone going to Ireland to study. I invite you to another drink. We'll drink for Ireland this time. It is regrettable really. It is Scotland then. I was about to give him the address of friends of mine in Dublin, but that's of no good to him as he's going to Scotland. I don't know anybody there. In Scotland they don't like lies. They can't stand them at all. It would not benefit you to invent the greatest and most beautiful stories. It will mean nothing to them if you have Picasso's talent in drawing or if you write poetry like Dante. In Scotland they are realistic to the extreme. Nothing satisfies them except truths, no matter how harsh they are. If you are going there forget about stories and poetry and fill your pockets with money. It was a good chance to meet him anyway. Tell him that. I could see he was a stranger, so I came to talk to him. These cities are cruel to strangers. No one will talk to you, but Ireland is different. It's a different world altogether. 'Tell him that.'

7

The Book of the Dead

H is first impression was that for one reason or another, they had all absented themselves from school that morning. On his way to the classroom Abdul Hafidh had stopped off at the staff room as usual to pick up the attendance register, then walked down a long corridor, the walls of which were covered with news-sheets and pupils' drawings. When he saw that the door at the end of the corridor was closed, and heard no sound from his students, none of the noise and quarrels that he was accustomed to hearing every morning, he realised that the devils must have invented some excuse to take the day off. He ought therefore to go back to the board of governors and firmly demand that they find a solution to this perpetual truancy. And he vowed to record their absence as inexcusable, whatever reasons or pretexts they might offer. Just to exclude any possibility of doubt, he opened the classroom door and closed it again without so much as a glance inside. He sensed a faint movement coming from somewhere so he opened the door again, and discovered to his immense surprise that the students were all there, sitting well-behaved in their places with their notebooks open before them, and silently engrossed in reading or writing, as if they had suddenly been transformed into adults.

Abdul Hafidh entered the classroom speechless with astonishment. He looked around him. First, he looked for a man from the Ministry lying in wait for him, for there could be no explanation for the amazing calm pervading the classroom other than that an inspector from the Ministry of Education had arrived before him. He must have chosen this early hour of the day for his hour of inspection in order to embarrass him in front of his pupils and note down his one failure to arrive punctually. But a glance at his watch assured him that he was right on time. So he lifted his head defiantly, and prepared to confront the inspector, whom he judged to be standing by the blackboard. There was nobody there. What sort of malicious joke was this? He knew only too well the cat and mouse games which the inspectors played with such finesse. He walked around the blackboard and the table, thinking that the inspector might be hiding behind one of them. But no one was there.

For a moment he stood still, astonished, unable to make sense of what was happening. He surveyed the room – perhaps some strange event had occurred – but no, everything was in order. Each boy was sitting in the place which had been his since the beginning of the year; the window was the same window through which one could see the cherry tree standing proud and splendid, covered with fresh new leaves; the paintings on the wall were the same primitive and clumsy paintings that he was used to seeing; the blackboard had not been moved a fraction of an inch from its usual position; the class was his usual class, and the pupils were his pupils, with grey and pallid complexions.

He had not taken the wrong road that morning, and by mistake entered a school in another country, town or planet. Everything in the classroom was normal and familiar, except for this strange calm, the like of which he had never experienced before in any class during his lifelong career as a teacher. Then his attention was drawn to a chair at the back of the class which was usually empty. On it was a pupil who normally sat in front of him, on the first chair to the left. He was about to ask him the reason for this change, when he glimpsed the pupil's former seat. He suddenly discovered that it was calmly occupied by ... a sorcerer! He beseeched God to save him from the devil. It was undoubtedly a sorcerer, disguised as a girl, who had come impudently, discourteously and indiscreetly to defy universal standards of conduct by sitting there in front of him. Horrified, he looked at her sitting among his male students as if she were one of them, and had known them for a long time. She was confident, as if it were quite normal and natural for a girl to be in a boys' school, in a class exclusively for boys. Terror-stricken, he went on staring at her as if he were witnessing a murder in his classroom. How could he, Abdul Hafidh, comprehend such a scene? He knew beyond doubt that it was a boys', not a girls' school. All the teachers were men, and all the pupils male. How, then, had this girl managed to sneak into the classroom, and by what right was she sitting there in front of him? He would not allow anyone to take him by surprise like this. He had woken up that morning, prayed, eaten his breakfast, shaved, and after correcting his pupils' exercise books, had put on his coat and come to school, never dreaming that he would come to find a sorcerer disguised as a girl, siting insolently before him and apparently unaware of what went thought his mind. He had always believed that girls had other lessons to learn, under the guidance of teachers of their own sex, in their own single-sex schools, schools with big iron gates and high walls, that guarded

52

their secrets well. What was taught to boys was something different, it was exclusively a man's affair and a woman should be ashamed and reluctant to listen to it, not defy all standards of decency by sitting in the boys' classroom, listening to what they listen and writing what they write and taking the same exams. The girl must have cheated her way into the school or climbed in through the window. There had to be some insidious scheme behind all this. If he should allow himself to treat her in the same way as he dealt with the boys it would be a grave and sinful crime for which he would be taken to court.

Bewilderment and fear overcame him, but he took care to hide it from his students. He drew himself up, frowned and addressed her in a cold and formal manner.

'Stand up.'

She stood up and to his dismay he saw she was a woman of about the same height as himself, her bosom fully developed and her hair dark and long, a woman in the prime of life. What a shame! She should by now be living the life of a married woman, in the home of her husband, not mixing with schoolboys who had just reached the age of puberty. There must be a plot behind it.

'Your name?'

Before she could reply, the boy who had let her have his chair volunteered to answer on her behalf.

'Sir her name is Zahra.'

The boy's intervention offended him and to add to his dismay he noticed that the boy looked like a pigmy, shabbily dressed, his teeth yellow and decayed. He realised that it must have been this boy who had smoked the cigarettes whose ends he habitually found on the floor. Losing patience, he repeated the question ignoring what the boy had just said:

'Your name?'

'Zahra Abdul Salam.'

Her voice was charged with defiance and pride. What sort of man was this Abdul Salam who allowed his daughter to go out and take up with boys instead of staying in the 'matrimonial home'? What sort of father was he to indulge in such permissiveness?

He looked her up in the register; her name was there, but written in pencil rather than printed. He felt confused: the school governors must therefore know. They were undoubtedly partners in a conspiracy against him. Abdul Hafidh thought that of all his enemies it was the inspectors who bore a grudge against him. They were bent on destroying him by obstructing his due promotion or transferring

53

him from one school to another. Now it seemed that they could think of nothing better than to bring this girl to his class, thus violating universal moral standards. Nobody else could be the target of this hideous plot. Nobody but him.

He even forgot which lesson he had prepared for his students – was it Arabic or religious instruction? With trembling fingers he held a piece of chalk, and absent-mindedly writing the date, it occurred to him that they were in the seventies, that more than twenty years had elapsed since he had first begun teaching. He suddenly felt very weary, and slumped on to his chair. He noticed that the girl was still standing, so he motioned to her with a gesture meant for her to leave, or sit down, disappear or die. But she quietly sat down and, lifting her little head, gazed stubbornly at him. Meanwhile, he decided to submit his resignation that very day, without any hesitation or regrets.

He sat silent, buried his head in his hands, forgot about the eyes that were fixed on him, and thought of this heresy, this fallacy and fire. All his life he had been pious, honest and straightforward observing the limits set by God. He had always believed that a woman was to be honoured, that her place should be at home, away from the eyes of men, that the devil would be the vicious third party of any encounter between a man and a woman. Consider then the encounter of one woman with thirty, nay a thousand men. As a result the devil would invade the universe, disaster would befall the world and the Resurrection would be imminent.

To be free to think he dictated to the students an exercise in sentence analysis. The lesson would soon be over and he would go to the governors to submit his resignation, for this was precisely what they were so desperate to achieve. But he would not hand them this opportunity on a plate. The wisest thing to do would be to frustrate them, to leave them with a thorn in the flesh. As soon as the lesson ended he stormed off to see the headmaster who, he thought, would fabricate some sort of a story. The headmaster's version was that the girl's father was a government employee, who had been transferred to this suburban district which had only one school. In order to secure the girl's further education they had decided that it would be within the law to accept her and the Ministry had agreed. But he knew all the tricks of the younger generation which had all too hastily and arbitrarily been placed in high educational and administrative positions. He would fight them single-handed and show them what a sordid affair it was.

The next day he decided to ignore the girl. The most telling of all attitudes would be to take no account of her and to give his lecture as though she were not there. He resolved to ask her no questions, not to touch her exercise book, and to register neither her presence nor her absence, to disregard and ignore her until she felt ashamed of herself or shamed those who had brought her to the school, so that she would go back whence she came defeated and humiliated.

He entered the classroom, and was amazed to observe the quiet and orderly behaviour of his students, which the day before he had believed to be an exceptional situation. No skirmishes, quarrels or noise. The boys seemed to have come from another planet, a planet without stables, forests, monkeys or sand. Their faces were clean and bright. They were well groomed, their hair neatly combed and their clothes smart. They had gone from rags to riches, their ramshackle homes had become palaces, their ignorant mothers cultured ladies of high society. He started to contemplate them as if he were seeing them for the first time. A new spirit and perfume infused the classroom. He noticed also that they were all paying attention to the lesson for the first time, and that they had all done their homework. What an enormous change it was. He wondered what miracle had brought about this great transformation. As the lesson progressed, Abdul Hafidh became increasingly aware of the students' astonishing improvement. Even the most stupid and absent-minded of them was now glowing with enthusiasm and attentiveness, as if sudden genius had descended upon him. They were inspired and replied to his questions with flowing and eloquent answers. They expressed themselves powerfully, in a manner he had never seen before. And he himself felt for the first time the importance of the lecture he was giving. They listened to him, earnestly following his words, as if what he was saying had assumed world-wide significance, as if he possessed the secrets of the universe. This was something he had never experienced in his twenty years of teaching. Suddenly and unconsciously he caught himself looking at the girl, wondering what kind of infernal power she possessed. The enchantress was innocently sitting in her place, unaware of her magical powers, as if the wonderful changes in his students had occurred without any effort on her part. From what exotic country did she come to achieve what all the educational books, all the ministries, the states and their fleets had failed to do? They were mere schoolboys, haunted by fiendish spirits which drove them to be quarrelsome and belligerent, yet here she came to transform the devils in them into human beings, their rags into riches, their stupidity into genius, their ugliness into good looks.

It became clear to him that if she should throw a stick on to the ground, the stick would turn into a snake, that she could draw flocks of birds or streams of rabbits from her sleeve or bring about any miracle she wanted. There must be something in her which surpassed his imagination and his feeble capacity for reasoning.

He continued to look at her, hoping to find an answer to his bewilderment. Everything about her was normal and it was clear from the first glance that she had to be Libyan.

There was something fundamentally Libyan about her, something which was visible in every feature of her face – a light sallowness, which all the signs of health and well-being could not conceal. Despite this sallowness, however, her face was radiant with an unassuming beauty like that of a palm-bordered oasis.

There was nothing in her looks to betray her latent powers, but still he sensed something strangely devilish about her, something that did not belong in this world. His wandering eyes lighted on the bottom of her chair whereupon he discovered that her feet were like donkey hooves. But before emitting a scream that would shatter the walls of the school, he realised that they were her own feet and that what he saw was simply the heels of her shoes. He was afraid that she had read his thoughts and would angrily transform him into a stick, a tree, a frog or a mewing cat. He called upon God to drive away these tortuous images and, closing the book on religion, hurried off before the lesson was due to end.

Arriving home he was still trembling with a strange fear, as if he had committed a crime, and would be severely punished. The image of the donkey hooves was following him; even in his sleep. Sometimes he saw her with two fearful bat's wings, sometimes as a fire-breathing dragon, or brandishing the claw of a mythical monster, demonically pursuing him everywhere. He caught himself fearfully repeating her name out loud. After the dawn prayer he discovered that he had brought her exercise book with him along with the other students'. He sat down to leaf through it with trembling fingers. Contrary to his expectations, there was nothing strange in her exercise book, no weird ciphers or hieroglyphics such as one finds in the Book of the Dead. Her exercise book was quite ordinary except for her neat and beautiful handwriting. Although her work was very good, he decided to bring her down a peg, so he took a pen and with childish stubbornness gave her lower marks than she really deserved. He would fight her, and not be intimidated by all the kings at her disposal. In the classroom the next day he awaited her reaction, when he thought it would be to transform him into a rat, a cat or a frog. But he would not give in or falter, as it was a matter of principle and pride, of life and death. She was busy comparing her exercise book with that of her neighbour, when she made to say something, but he motioned her to keep silent. Let her cry or commit suicide by throwing herself out of the window, he would not allow her to trick and would fight her black magic until the end.

With this in mind, he continued to tease her, seizing upon any opportunity to rebuke her and giving her the lowest possible grades however well she did her homework. In return she seemed to be ignorant of his competitive attitude, and sat calmly in her place, filling the classroom with her warm perfume as if the matter was of no concern to her, thus making him think that she was contriving some sinister deed against him. Any day now he would witness this horrible deed; what had been the school would be a heap of ashes, the students would be suddenly transformed into monkeys, or he would wake up to find himself turned into a rabbit, a hedgehog or a pig. But the days passed, and no great disaster struck. Nevertheless, he went on expecting something of the order of an earthquake or the Resurrection to take place. Then one day she did not come to the lesson. He felt that the very basis on which he had built his life was collapsing. The magic which had filled the classroom with its perfume had disappeared; the boys were ugly, poor and stupid again and they seemed to have returned to their old, bad ways. The classroom was dark and dim, for the sun which has risen in it had gone out. He had always imagined that the girl's disappearance from the school would be a great victory which would fill his heart with unalloyed joy and contentment, but the victory which he had nervously fought to win was a hollow one. On the contrary the sadness tightened his heart and his mouth became dry as if full of ashes. He had lost something essential to his life, something which had filled his heart with sprightliness and defiance, and for the first time he began to question himself and was filled with remorse; a spider was weaving a cobweb inside his heart.

He had been extremely hard on her, groundlessly imagining her to be a mermaid or a dragon when as a matter of fact she was simply an innocent little girl. Had he married earlier he would by now have had a daughter of her own age. The classroom was sad to contemplate. It was mere wasteland inhabited by those fiendish boys, and he seriously thought of going out looking for her to ask her to forgive him and to beg her father to bring her back to school, promising sincerely to treat her like a princess or a queen. He decided to do this at the first opportunity.

Fortunately enough she came back the next day. The pupils regained their health and good looks; her warm perfume filled the air; a sun was again transplanted into the centre of the classroom. Happiness was a flock of sparrows flying to his heart, which was like a dying and withered tree that put forth fresh, green branches. For the first time teaching seemed to Abdul Hafidh the most beautiful of all vocations, coming to the class was an ever-renewed feast, not a tiresome duty. The girl was no sorceress or dragon, but a beautiful and clever girl. He treated her kindly and generously gave her excellent grades. If she was one minute late, he would start to worry, and as soon as she left he would feel eager to see her the next day. He unconsciously started to take the utmost care of his appearance. He even put on every day the suit which he had reserved for special feast-days, and he adopted the habit of shaving every morning instead of once or twice a week.

He was rediscovering himself. His age, which he had thought to be swiftly approaching the age of retirement, was in fact only five or six years past forty. He had always felt older than he was, mainly because he had started work at a very early age. But he was still in his prime, despite his ageing wife and the children who swarmed about the house like ants. Life, he observed now, was still before him like a wide open way with all its riches. He had been unjustly judging himself and his youth when he had imagined that he was an old man. He even remembered that his grandfather had married for the seventh or eighth time at the age of seventy, something that made him feel even younger, like a boy of the same age as his pupils, with new blood running through his veins like sap. A carpet, beautifully ornamented with boats, gardens, sparrows and butterflies extended between his house and the school, a carpet on which he gracefully walked every morning and which led him to her as she quietly sat on her chair, lighting up the room like a lamp. As soon as he saw her a sweet numbness swept through his body. The circle of her magic, he thought, had enlarged to include him and the students. The lecture would be sheer happiness and the time would pass quickly to make him impatiently eager to see her again the next day. In the meantime, and for reasons beyond his comprehension, teacher Abdul Hafidh grew impatient – and felt increasingly hemmed-in at home. He could not bear to stay indoors, caught between walls, under walls, under roofs or behind closed doors. He often went for solitary walks in the open, to the spacious squares and public gardens and along the shores, deeply immersed in thoughts about this girl who had unexpectedly entered his life and his classroom, this girl to whom he was strangely drawn by something which he did not dare to acknowledge. She was like a strange creature emerging from under heaps of snow to defy beyond reason the traditions and ethics in which he believed, and to which he had dedicated his life. But he must not recognise his feelings, believe in or confess them, for the catastrophe which he had so long expected would then be unleashed. He had seen her every morning, quietly sitting there, innocently oblivious of the violent struggle taking place within him, of the secret links attaching him to her, and of the bottomless chasm into which he would fall, should he once obey the call of his burning heart. He had gone on in his ash-covered oblivion until this young girl had arrived to sweep away the dense piles of ashes and set his heart fiercely glowing. The worst thing was that he began to see her in his dreams, not as a fire-breathing dragon or a mythical creature with bat's wings, but as a young female, beautiful, seductive, and light-giving. They met in an open space, as if they were Adam and Eve suddenly descending to the earth to join each other after years of solitary wandering. In his dreams their meeting was so passionate, so delectable and yet so awful and scandalous that he would wake up frightened, and call upon God for forgiveness. He would then go to school confused and timid, with unsure steps, and unable to look at her or the others, as if they would catch him red-handed committing the most outrageous of deeds.

As the days passed, he grew more and more convinced that he had been the victim of a plot hatched in secret, that he had been right in his initial belief that the girl was a devil lying in wait for him. Her appearance, he concluded, was not as innocent as it had seemed. She was intent on catching him in her deadly net and breathing her black magic into his breast. She was artfully seducing him so that he would blindly fall down a dark, fearful well of debauchery, filth and atheism. This devilish feeling which had spread like an evil plant in his chest, against all reason, logic, tradition, morals and virtue, and had assumed the form of a mocking head peering out of the snow, had not grown by accident. From the start he had expected the worst of calamities to drag him into an abyss, all because of this girl who was robbing him of his virtues and making the pious and honest teacher that he was, into a terrible and shameless image of a man devoid of all good behaviour, honour and virtue, a wicked man obsessed by a little girl who would be the same age as his daughter if he had one. By what fiendish means was a girl, to whom he gave religious instruction, dragging him into the most evil situation. His salvation, he determined, lay in resisting her magic by a magic stronger than hers. He hysterically started to leaf through thick, yellowing volumes, in the hope that he would find something capable of deadening the effect of the book which she had brought from the world of ghosts and the dead.

To the astonishment of his wife and children, he turned the house upside down. No trace of her magic could be found. He even took an axe and dug up the front porch, thinking that they might have hidden it there. He tore the covers off the school textbooks, hoping to find it in the form of a tiny pinpoint. He was suspicious enough to shave his head completely, to make sure that they had not hidden her magic there in something as minute as a grain of sand. His suspicions were confirmed when the headmaster warned him of his possible dismissal from work. His wife took his children and went to her parents' house, and the students rudely made fun of him. He had exposed them; they had plotted against him and had used the girl to ruin his life. His wife, the students, the headmaster, the teachers, the government inspectors, were all partners in this plot. Nothing would quench his thirst for revenge except to set his home, the school and the Ministry on fire, and Abdul Hafidh immediately set about fulfilling this mission.

8

Never Seen a River

There was a vacant chair at one of the few tables scattered on the pavement. He asked permission to join a man who sat drinking coffee, and threw himself down. He was tired. The waiter came and he ordered a cup of coffee.

He lit a cigarette and gazed dreamily at the street, which filled with the roar of traffic. For a moment he imagined that the street had been transformed into a river, the streams of cars into boats carrying lovers, slowly gliding downstream. On the far side he saw the moon glowing gold, lighting the blue of the river with fiery tongues. He saw himself sitting in a shady grove on the bank. Grasses and roses grew at this feet, butterflies and sparrows hovered near him, and all around were flowering trees. Beneath the trees were dozens of tables at which sat men and women, whispering to each other and exchanging toasts. He filled his lungs with the scent of roses and rapturously let himself be carried away by the sweet music coming from nearby.

He discovered that just beside him was a tree – a tree with a thick trunk covered with unopened buds. He was sitting under the very tree where he used to wait for his sweetheart, whom he expected any minute. But he heard a rustling sound, and as he raised his head, he saw that the tree had become a man, whom he recognised as the waiter bringing his coffee. He cursed him under his breath, this waiter who had caused the abrupt disappearance of boats, lovers, roses, sparrows and music. He looked to either side to determine whether one of the people sitting wearily in their chairs drinking coffee, had perhaps also seen the river. But they just sat there with blank expressions, dull and withdrawn, as if someone had just heaped ashes on their faces and clothes. He was sure that none of them had ever seen a river in his life. Once again he closed his eyes, trying to forget them and go back to the river all alone, where to meet his sweetheart, who would certainly be bathing naked in the water. But his daydream was spoiled by the man next to him, who slurped with every sip of coffee. His beloved, for whom he sat waiting under the tree, would never come! He looked angrily at the man; he had been transformed into a camel. He chuckled to himself;

how quickly these people turn into camels as soon as they drink coffee! He felt his neck, and decided that the man next to him had turned into a camel because he had not seen a river. Oh Lord, when shall I ever see this cursed river?

His appetite gone, he left the coffee untouched, and thought of his mother. She has a long neck as well. And every morning she sits on a cushion, craning her neck to see across the housetops, spying on relatives and neighbours. With a beady eye she peers into kitchen cupboards, searching among the crockery, under chairs and beds and in the stuffing of pillows, for a good little girl who might be a suitable bride for her son.

For the old woman was growing anxious seeing that her son was becoming no more than a stranger to her, some unknown other, a son distraught with anxiety, preoccupied, hardly talking or eating. Even his sleep scarcely passed undisturbed; he would leave his bed to walk around the house, as if his body was haunted by a devilish spirit.

So the old mother realised that the boy would be lost should she not with all speed find him a wife. He was aware of his mother's feelings. But....

'If you were a real mother you would get me a river instead of a wife.'

He laughed feebly. How can you blame a woman who has never in her life seen a river?

But the camel who sat drinking coffee next to him with elongated neck and the upper lip slit into two halves, looked him up and down and enquired in camel language if the conversation was directed at him. Anger welled in him; once more he felt certain that the beloved of his heart who swam naked in the river, had decided to desert him forever. He pretended to return the greeting of a man who passed by at a distance. The camel then drew in his neck and continued to drink coffee.

He had told the old mother that it was a question, not of a woman but of a river. But she did not seem to understand. How could he get it into her head that his crisis did not depend on her finding him by chance a good girl in one of the cracks of the old houses. If it had been just that, everything would have run smoothly since the first day of his seeing the daughter of their neighbour, the grocer.

On that day the grocer's daughter was smiling at him as she looked through the partly opened door. He thought then that all the rivers of the world had their hidden sources in that neighbour's house. But this happy spell proved to be short-lived, for the next day

62

they drove a stake firmly into the courtyard and by way of punishment, hung a rope round her neck and fastened her to the stake. The girl instantly turned into a sheep. At night her sad bleating could be heard in the desolate town. He came to realise that all the houses that in different parts of the town were set securely in the ground, were turned at night time into stables. For in every such house was a young girl who one day tried to satisfy her curiosity by peeping through the door to find out the only thing she really wanted to know – if there was a river flowing by the door. On daring to do so she was shackled by a rope to a stake in the courtyard.

His mother did not understand this; she did not know that girls in their town were at sunset transformed into sheep, that men were transformed into camels as they drank coffee. This for the simple reason that not one of them tried to see a river before it was too late.

He himself was bewildered, unable to find a reason for the anxiety that took hold of him as if an unlimited number of black ants was chasing him everywhere. A heavy cloud of melancholy would settle on his chest every evening and he would feel that there was no more air in the world, that he was going to die of suffocation. Ghosts and insomnia every night and terrifying nightmares. And every morning a stale bitter taste as though lemons had been squeezed in his mouth. His appetite for food, his drive for work were gone. Not to speak of reading; for the newspapers which he had been addicted to were unbearable, as if scorpions and beetles would jump out at his face the moment he started to leaf through the first pages. He did not even dare to approach the many radios at home for fear that his face would be scalded with a boiling broth should he touch them. Finally, that feeling of disgust that filled him and made him shun the company of others, or engaging them in conversation. He was forever unable to find an explanation for what had happened to him, until one day, just like that, an idea as swift as lightning crossed his mind. He was sitting one evening as usual in the café. He suddenly realised that he had never seen a river in his life. It is true that he had read or heard about rivers, that he had seen films showing rivers or telling stories about them, but he had not actually seen a real river with his own eyes. A firm conviction then started to grow in him, the conviction that the suffering in his life was due only to his not having seen a river. The ghosts that haunted him at night, the swarms of black ants in the daytime, and the bitter taste of lemon were nothing more than the result of his not having seen a flowing river. It would be a different matter if the village where he spent his childhood years was not planted in the heart of the desert but by one of the rivers; or if the town to which he had moved later had been situated on the banks of a river. For the beloved of his heart, the girl who inspired him with illusions of a tree under which he sat waiting for her to come naked out of the water, would not have deserted him. The world would have been vibrating with singing, dancing and music, and life would have been meaningful. It just happened; a strange feeling took on the power of a conviction that life without a river is no life, that a man who has not at some time lived by a river is no man, that it is not in vain that God created Paradise with rivers flowing through it, that it was only the lack of rivers that gave its name to Hell.

From that day on he was convinced that he could explain every phenomenon in his town. This haphazard conglomeration of bad taste around him no more aroused his anger or bewilderment. How could he flare up at the inoffensive waiter, when he knew that this ill-fated waiter had never seen a river in his life? And how could he feel upset about the aggressive mobs who filled the cinemas with noise and obscene comments, when he knew that this wretched crowd had never sat on the bank of a river to exchange toasts with their women? How could he be angered when he saw a youngster driving a car in such a crazy way that it looked like a bull running amok, when he knew that this boy had never had the chance of being on a boat bearing him gently on the river? And how could he feel sad about the degrading standards of radio announcers, journalists, musicians and songwriters when he knew that they all had never seen a river in their lives?

He stubbed out his cigarette and looked with dismay at the cup of cold coffee which he had not touched, and thought that the street really should turn into a river. Everything, then, would be changed; the man next to him would not turn into a camel as soon as he drank coffee; the beloved who delighted in swimming naked in the river, in the moonlight, would keep her date, the neighbour's daughter would not turn into a sheep, her bleating would not disturb the city at night.

He then thought that these people should look for their own salvation. It would not matter if the river they sought was of the smallest size and magnitude. A small part of a river, to be taken from one of the many that run throughout the world would be enough, a trivial part that would cost next to nothing. But he realised that it was impossible, although he was convinced that somebody must recognise the importance of having a river in one's life. People must know the tragedy of having to live all the time without seeing a river. Perhaps one day they would set out on a march to dig deep into the bowels of the earth and make for themselves the sought-for river. The urgent thing, however, was that he should seek an outlet for himself and get away to see a river before it was too late.

The camel next to him was widening his cleft upper lip, lengthening his neck, and smiling. He was welcoming a man who had just come up. He invited the man to sit, and ordered him a cup of coffee. The first sip and the man turned into a camel.

For some reason he himself felt that he would soon be transformed into a camel, that his neck would grow longer and longer and his upper lip be split into two.

He did not know where to turn.

Should he scream?

Should he ask somebody for help?

He looked to either side. His heart was overwhelmed with genuine terror. The whole world seemed to him to be full of camels. He threw his cup of coffee into the air, pulled himself up quickly from where he sat, took off his slippers and put them under his arm, and dashed off without knowing in which direction he was going. He was running down the middle of the street, running away head over heels, unconscious of whatever might happen. He was running, running and he would not stop running. He would ignore sunrise and sunset, day and night, hunger and thirst. He would pay no attention to any mountains, rocks, difficult terrain or seas of sand that might crop up on his way. He would cross them all and would not stop running. He would run and run until he reached it. For there must be a river somewhere; he would not stop until he came to it, and then he would throw himself upon it, thus putting an end to all those years he had spent in constant anguish at never seeing a river.

9

Love Me Tonight

The odour assailed him instantly. He had paid for a ticket and crossed a long corridor, then slunk past a red curtain which covered the entrance into the warmth of the hall within.

He stood there for a moment to take off his coat and wipe the drops of rain which clung to his hair. He waited for his eyes to get accustomed to the gloom. The same odour rushed over him again: a mingled smell of perfume, perspiration, tobacco smoke and wine. It was now part of the place, it had hung there and accumulated, growing stale, clinging to the ceiling and becoming increasingly pungent. The smell aroused in him a desire to escape at once from this place and return to the street outside, to the lights, the sky and fresh air. Also to return to the hotel where members of the delegation, of whom he was one, were staying. He had waited until they all went to bed after a tiring journey from Tripoli before feeling confident enough to venture out.

A drum, being played somewhere in the night-club, seemed to be calling out to him. The sound of its beat appeared as if it was carried on the air waves from a distant place, moving towards him and calling him by his name, Abdullah. The drum was speaking in a mysterious language whose symbols he could not decipher, nor discover its secrets. Yet something deep within him recognised it, comprehended its message and was able to respond to it. All the other musical instruments accompanying this drum paled in comparison, as it continued to throb out its messages. It was as if an African tribe was communicating with one of its sons who had strayed and got lost in the jungle. He was about to fall prey to some wild ravenous beasts, so they were sending out a warning, and guiding his way back home to safety.

His eyes were getting used to the darkness. There was no jungle, no African tribe, nor any ferocious animals. The night-club was no different from any he had seen before. It was elegant, very sumptuous and glamorous; not so much a night-club, but more like the reception hall of an extremely wealthy man. Everything in it was glittering and glowing under the dim lights which were placed strategically in all corners. Even the carpets, curtains, décor, marble pillars and the tables at which the customers sat were magnificent. The clientele themselves glowed iridescently as if some phosphorous dust had been sprinkled all over their heads and clothes. They were all sitting at their tables in silence, concentrating on the music as if in a state of prayer. They didn't seem to be watching a show or listening to a band, but as if they were participating in an act of worship which demanded supplication and reverence. He also noticed that contrary to what he was used to seeing in most night-clubs, not one customer was drunk or moved unsteadily amongst the tables. Every one of the customers was sober, glittering phosphorously under the lights.

A waiter moved forward to take his coat and usher him to a table he had chosen for him. He was wearing a suit which looked more like a period costume. His demeanour and manner of speech were impeccable as befitting a most exclusive salon. He didn't look like an ordinary waiter, but more like a liveried Master of Ceremonies at a royal banquet. Everything about the place aroused Abdullah's suspicions. He had crept stealthily out of the hotel under cover of darkness to indulge in a few drinks which he longed for, away from the prying eyes of the other inquisitive members of the delegation. He now found himself inside a strange world the likes of which he had never encountered previously. The only thing that worried him was a scandal should he be found out by the rest of the delegates who, like him, were attending a conference the following day.

He wondered what the place actually was, perhaps it was not a night-club at all. It was definitely not the palatial mansion of a wealthy man he had strayed into by mistake. He had paid for a ticket and a clear illuminated sign outside advertised this establishment as a night-club. What was it then? Perhaps it was the den of a gang of criminals who employed such a grand manner to trap their victims! The silence which reigned all over the assembled people, above which nothing was heard apart from the sound of the music, was eerie. It indicated that something out of the ordinary was about to take place and they were all holding their breath in anticipation of a strange spectacle. Perhaps a Samurai warrior would emerge from behind one of the pillars, unsheathe a sword hanging from his belt and commit hari-kiri in the traditional Japanese way. Perhaps one of the customers sitting at his table would suddenly leap up, kiss his lady companion, then draw a gun out of his pocket, aim it at her forehead then shoot her whereupon she would slump down dead on the floor. Or a similar violent act which would fill them with terror. Why not leave immediately and save his skin before it was too late?

68

But the magical irresistible beat of the drum continued, even after the dance show came to an end and it was the turn for a singer to appear on stage.

All that mattered to him was that beat, the likes of which he could not recall hearing anywhere else. No other rendering or singing had so captivated his senses like this drum, played by an old negro who artfully and skilfully employed it as an instrument for relating all the tales, poetry and legends contained in Africa. He was deeply immersed in these ancient visions awakened in him by this playing, as he greedily drained his third drink, when he suddenly discovered that the place had abruptly and rapidly emptied of all customers! His heart missed a beat as he looked all around him fearfully, but there was no one around except for a few waiters scattered here and there. One of them, the same waiter who met him at the door and led him to his table, was standing nearby, looking at him and smiling malevolently. The game was now over and the trap was sprung! The scandal he had feared about to happen. Indeed not only a scandal but even the threat of murder! He would be discovered, an unidentified victim, in a den of sin and inequity.

His reputation had always remained unblemished back in his home town. He was known to follow the Holy scriptures both in word and deed. All the people who knew him addressed him by the respectful and distinguished title of 'Sheikh Abdullah'. What would they think of him now. What legacy would he leave his young daughter and his son, who was ten years old, soon to reach manhood? He cursed his weakness which drove him to this place. He realised that the first thing he must now do was to muster all his strength and make a dash for the door. He must attempt to save himself, rather than submit to this fate. He was poised for flight when a swift glance in the direction of the dance floor surprised him greatly. All the customers were crowded in that space!

His heart resumed beating. It dawned on him that it was now the turn for the customers to dance for a while. He breathed a great sigh of relief and scolded himself for thinking ill of the waiter who was not smiling gloatingly, but amiable. The dancing had now started and all he had to do was to join the others and follow suit. There was no reason now for fear, suspicion or thoughts of flight. Everything around him promised an enjoyable and entertaining evening.

The sound of the drum was still reverberating against the walls and ceiling of the hall, inviting him to the delights of the world. All he had to do was get up and dance as no one had ever danced before. Not only dance, but hold a dialogue with the rhythmic beat of the drum, transported by perfume-laden winds from the heart of Africa. It would be his only means of communicating with this drum, to which he felt bound by old ties of friendship. He would relate to it through his dancing all the stories he had learnt from his grandmother as a child, growing up in a village on the edge of the desert. He would recount all his worries and sorrows and would not cease until he had completely freed himself of all the burdens that weighed him down. He would dance and dance until he collapses down with exhaustion!

He almost made his way to the dance floor only to realise in the nick of time that it would be useless. It had escaped his notice in the midst of all his musing that he had no partner to dance with. He also remembered that he had never been taught how to dance in the European fashion. In fact the very first time he had seen men and women dancing together was during his first visit abroad. How could he have failed to notice that he was the only unaccompanied person in that hall? The other clientele had naturally headed for the dance floor because that's what they'd been used to since childhood. None of them arrived at this place on his own, every man was accompanied by a woman and vice versa, consequently they danced together. He felt acutely embarrassed at being the odd one out. He was like a cripple, the blood in his veins turned into water and he was powerless to stand up or move his feet. He was certainly disabled and his only hope of recovery from the paralysis which afflicted him was to see another person on his own not participating in the dancing. One last sweeping glance around him dashed his hopes and increased his discomfort. He was the only person without a partner.

The waiter was still standing there, looking in his direction and smiling. He ordered another drink, hoping the waiter would go away. However, after fetching the drink, the waiter went back to his former place, turning towards him to smile now and again. The smile did not appear malicious or ingratiating, but it was derisive and scornful. Abdullah felt the situation getting increasingly embarrassing and the paralysis in his legs grew worse.

He felt like saying to the waiter:

'What's so amusing? You're just a waiter giving yourself airs and graces as if you were a royal Master of Ceremonies. What's so odd about a customer not taking part in the dancing? Haven't you seen this happen before? Perhaps you've discovered that I'm a visitor from Tripoli. What's so shameful about this? You are nothing but a royal fake, hiding your horns under a haze of phosphorous dust!

Tripoli is one of the greatest cities in the world. It has witnessed successive Roman, Greek and Arab civilisations. I am well aware of your countrymen's feelings of envy at our historical heritage. What's wrong with people who don't know how to dance? In my country we consider men and women dancing in public a disgrace. Where have you obtained such distorted facts about my nation? You who have been corrupted by a crumbling and decaying civilisation. What's wrong with the women in my country? They are sacrosanct and inviolable. You have to wash your mouth out in rosewater before speaking of their reputations. Do you want a life for them like that of the women in your country? Women whose femininity and humanity has no value. You want women to frequent clubs, cafés, dance in public, drink wine and accompany men everywhere ... do you call this freedom! Perhaps this is considered a virtue in your country. I see that you disapprove of our marriage custom. I know all the thoughts that go around in your head, whose brain cells have rotted with wine fumes. What's so disgusting about a man marrying a woman he had never seen until his wedding night? That's what happened to me when I got married. I accepted this person whom fate had led me to quite contentedly. How can you call this dreadful, you profligate, taking men to your wife's chamber each night after the show ends. How can we protect our sons and daughters from sin if we allow them licence to get acquainted, to mingle freely and indulge in love before marriage? What? Did I hear you mention love? What kind of 'love' is this that a man like you, devoting his life to debauchery, would like to sacrifice 'honour' for? Is there any love apart from the one you sell in dissolute shops which trade daily in this commodity? Isn't that the type of love you are referring to? No, my iridescent man, this love is what you keep to yourself and trade with as you please. I assure you that you will not succeed in corrupting us despite all the films of vice and profligacy which you send to us. We refuse to give up even one iota of the honour and virtue which distinguishes our lives and conduct. A man in my country still would not hesitate to kill his daughter immediately should he discover that she had succumbed to the corrupting influence of your films and magazines; or should she form a liaison with a man behind her family's back! Why are you looking at me with such astonishment? No, I have not yet lost my senses!'

'Bring me another drink and make it a double this time!' He called the waiter over so sharply that it startled the man, who hurried to his side.

The dancing was now over and people were returning to their

71

tables. The drum stopped playing. The compère announced a magician who hurried onto the stage. He immediately went into his act, pulling out handkerchiefs and a large number of doves out of his pockets. It so happened that when the customers returned to their tables, a young couple were sitting directly opposite Abdullah. He had probably given them a fleeting glance at the beginning of the evening, but only now did he become aware that they were not exactly adults, but teenagers, almost children. What else could he call a man of about eighteen or nineteen and a woman of a similar age but children?! How could he help but feel shocked and wonder at the motives of a father or mother who would allow such young people to attend a night-club at this hour of the night?

Abdullah devoted himself exclusively to the two young people. He gave up watching the magician and adjusted his seat so that he could observe no other spectacle but them. The girl was wearing a simple sky-blue dress whose hem just about covered her knees. The boy was wearing a full evening dark-coloured suit, exactly as if he were to anticipate his manhood. Apart from the glow of the phosphorescent dust which made everything around them sparkle and glow, there was nothing exceptionally exciting about them, apart from the fact that the girl was very pretty. Hers was the type of simple subdued beauty which reminded one immediately of the most beautiful poetry ever read, and the most beautiful music ever heard. It invoked all the most glorious scenes of sunrise, sunset, lakes and rivers which had held their spectator spellbound. Her face had an angelic aura, reminding one of the drawings in children's books. If he could think of a title for her, the one that most readily came to mind would be 'Cinderella'. She was indeed none other than this character, emerging straight out of the pages of a fairy story book.

The young man was indeed a child, with baby features except that he had a man's build and height. One could not help but imagine him as a knight riding astride a winged horse, which parted a path through the clouds as it rose high up into the air. The knight was on his way to abduct his lady love who was waiting for him on a high balcony bathed in moonlight, just as a scene from a young girl's fantasy.

Despite sitting close to them and being completely absorbed with them, he could not make out what the young lovers were whispering to each other. In fact they did not say much, being content with a single word, a murmur or a sign in order to be understood. They giggled and laughed, delighting in each others' mutual happiness. He watched them during moments when they were so completely wrapped up in each other, that it seemed as if a force had dismissed all other people away from the face of the earth and no one was left on it except for themselves. All the cities, oceans and forests on it were their sole exclusive domain. They would indeed be most surprised should they discover that this wasn't the fact and that they were not the only two people in the night-club, but that there were scores of other customers in it as well. The conjuror had now emptied his bag of all its tricks and was leaving the stage. The old negro appeared next, carrying his drum. He was accompanied by five dancing girls, scantily dressed in a few long coloured feathers. They launched into their dance routine, but the lovers soon returned to their absorption with each other. They laughed in mutual delight and wonder at everything that was going on around them, as if they were a prince and princess fresh out of the pages of a story book. Here they were discovering a new world which filled them with astonishment and curiosity. It was abundantly clear that their joy in each others' company knew no bounds. It seemed as if they had both suffered greatly in the past before they met. In fact Abdullah felt that the drum which had now resumed its pulsating rhythms, was telling their story. Apparently they were formerly two elderly people who had grown weary with time. The moment they met they changed into people in the full flush of youth! Should they get separated, even for an instant, they would return to their previous old decrepit selves. They might even evaporate into thin air and disappear completely off the face of the earth.

Abdullah believed what the drum was saying and could not imagine them staying away from each other. Should they get separated, they would do everything possible, even travelling from the furthest corner of the earth, to be with each other. Otherwise they would perish or melt away. Or they might find themselves being transformed by God into a rat, a rabbit, a tortoise or an ant. Their only hope of deliverance from such a fate would be to stay together constantly.

Abdullah began to realise that what he was watching was true love. The preconceptions he had formed in his mind about love began to disappear. He was now certain of the beauty and splendour of human emotions. He was utterly convinced that illness would never afflict anyone who had experienced such feelings. Such a person would never know poverty or hunger, indeed not even death itself. He was certain in his mind that even the rain which poured down outside would not dare drench their hair or clothes should they go outside, because it would know that they were in love. Neither

73

cold nor heat would bother them. No one would prevent them from entering any restaurant, café or place of entertainment, where they would be allowed to enjoy eating, drinking and watching free of charge. Moreover, they would not have to pay for transport or pay rent for the house they occupied. Indeed not pay for anything they bought from shops because they were in love!

Only now was he awakened to the tragedy of human existence without love. It was a calamity that he had spent a lifetime as a prisoner of an environment which regarded love as an obscenity. He had been conditioned to believe in this notion, and had not discovered its sham and falsehood until it was too late. It was only now that he realised the extent of the ugliness in his life. Not once during his lifetime had he exercised his human potential.

Long ago he had been transformed into a tortoise, an ant, a rat. He was certain that all the ailments which had afflicted him throughout his life: headaches, insomnia and fevers were caused because he had not loved. All his worries, misfortunes and sorrows took place because he had not loved. That was the reason he ran away from fights as a boy. When rainwater soaked him, when cold or scorching heat harmed him, when his boss at work had given him a written warning, when creditors demanded payment of debts: all these things occurred because he had not loved. Even when death itself comes to claim him, it would do so because Abdullah had lived most of his life without experiencing this kind of love.

For the first time he was aware that the years of his youth had slipped between his fingers like water. He had not known even one day of enjoyment. He led his life like an old man of a hundred! He was suddenly seized with real panic. Just at that moment a significant thought crossed his mind, something he had lived with all his life but only now made an impact upon him. Here in this night-club, in this foreign country, in the presence of the drum and the young lovers, only now did he become aware that not once during his forty years of age did he ever receive a love letter. If only he could have received a perfumed envelope containing a letter from a woman who loved him! Even if her love was untrue, even if it were a mere frivolity or an illusion, he would not have endured such suffering. It could have changed the entire course of his life. Fearing that someone might discover his secret, he peered around the place apprehensively, but nobody took any notice of him. Everyone was still covered in that iridescent dust. Men and women whispering to each other, sipping their drinks and watching the show. The young couple were still oblivious of the world around them, lost in their own private existence. He felt reassured that nobody knew his affairs. He suddenly woke up from the reverie when he heard someone call his name. He knew at once that it was none other than that evil drum which refused to let him be. It was now telling the story of a man who had wasted his life in vain. He had denied himself human needs and ignored his inner voice. He had submitted obediently to his society's oppressive tradition. To please this society he had worn a mask, mistaking it for a real face and had led his life on this basis. When he did wake up one day and realised that the mask wasn't real after all and wished to replace it with his real face, he discovered that he had none left at all. He knew at once that the drum was speaking of none other than himself, and that it was taunting him for each wasted day. It was exposing his secret to the world and showing him up naked. Will this accursed drum never cease tormenting him and hold its tongue forever? But the drum went on beating, quickening its tempo then slowing down, growing to a crescendo, then calming down to a whisper, ascending and descending. He felt it lift him up bodily and fling him through the ceiling, then bring him crashing down upon the floor like a limp rag. He tried to close his eyes to avoid seeing it, and shut his ears to avoid hearing it, but the beat invaded all his being and aroused in him endless pangs of anguish.

For some inexplicable reason, all his rage and disappointment turned against the young couple, as if they alone were responsible for his life-long suffering and misery. He had always thought of himself as a successful man, attaining through his own efforts an enviable position in society. He had been selected as a representative of his country at important international conferences. This evening, a young couple lacking any decency, sensitivity or decorum had torn off all the clothing which covered him. They demolished all the protective defences he had erected around himself, only to discover that these measures were but an illusion and a lie. If he had a gun in his pocket, he would not have hesitated for one moment to shoot them and watch them die!

He addressed them mentally:

'What bad luck brought you here today? Why didn't you find some other place to go to except this particular night-club? Why did you choose this table directly opposite mine? Why didn't you pick another night to come to this place, so you can indulge in this debauchery as you please without considering others? Perhaps one or both of you are party to this plot against me in this city, where I'm spending my first night. Hasn't one of you got a strict father, who would arrive immediately here and drag you outside, punish you severely and forbid you from ever seeing the other person again?

The young couple stood up. He realised that it was once more the turn of the customers to dance. The young man encircled the girl's tender pliant waist gently with his arm, as if afraid to snap it. Every male went with his female, but he remained on his own.

'No waiter, don't expect me to hide under the table or conceal myself behind one of the curtains! I have nothing to hide. The drum has revealed everything about me! As for you, young man, you may take your girl and swagger around, full of conceit and vanity. It doesn't matter. Let each one of you dancers embrace his lady and dance. As for me, I have lost the use of my legs for some time now. Don't you realise that I can only crawl!'

The thought made him laugh. His laughter rose to a guffaw which startled the waiter standing near him, and he promptly moved away. Abdullah continued to watch the young dancers with curiosity and fascination. 'Cinderella' had submitted to her prince and laid her head upon his shoulder, his eyes closed too. She lifted her head up towards him with her eyes still closed. He did likewise. They moved their heads closer until their features mingled together. Their hair, eyes and noses merged until they were no longer distinguishable. The blue of her dress blended in with the dark colour of his suit. Their lips sealed together, their bodies sank into each other as if they were one. He, too, lost himself in them. He became a third entity permeated within them. He was no longer conscious of the empty hall, the waiters or the drum. He was aware of nothing except for his soul which was joined to theirs. He began to understand that a young man kissing a young woman was not a crime punishable by death. Not a particle in his being felt outrage at what they were doing. On the contrary, it was now obvious that they were participating in a holy act. The kiss which joined them together physically and spiritually was a form of worship, which God sanctioned and in which the angels rejoiced. He had tried to lie to himself. He tried to convince himself that this was truly a breach of decent behaviour and morality. As a man of principle and an observer of honourable conduct he should disapprove of such an exhibition, but he could not. What he was witnessing was truly a form of prayer. If he should regret anything in this world, it must be that his life was wasted without such devotion.

The lovers finished their dance and returned to their table. They were leaning on each other playfully, their fingers intertwined, heads held close together. They whispered and laughed happily together. The display tested his patience to the utmost, and he wasn't too embarrassed to exclaim aloud :

'They're killing me!'

He was so overcome with misery that he no longer cared if people thought he was crazy. A woman's voice asked, her drunken breath hitting him in the face :

'Did you say anything?'

It was one of the showgirls. She had finished her number, got dressed and had occupied the only available seat next to him.

'No ... I was talking aloud to myself ... what's it to you? Why don't you mind your own business? Your dancing was fine anyway ... I was merely talking to myself.'

He was getting dangerously drunk.

'Someone wants to kill me tonight. You don't know this, but they want to destroy me! This does not concern you in any way, so why are you sitting here? Oh, no, no. I didn't come her tonight in search of a woman! I'm a man of principle! They don't allow me to ... forgive me ...'

She was watching him in astonishment. He continued:

'Shall I tell you a secret? Do you realise that I have never ever received a love letter? Have you ever met a man before who had never received a love letter, not once in all his life?! That's why one of them plans to kill me tonight. Perhaps they have indeed killed me. Look into my eyes, am I dead?! Alright? It's not your business, nor is it the business of this accursed drum to tell my life story to the world! I knew from the beginning that a plot was being hatched against me in this place. It never occurred to me that a real-life 'Cinderella' would kill me.'

The young lovers were preparing to depart. Abdullah reached for his glass but the woman prevented him:

'You've had enough, what's wrong with you? You're trembling!'

She reached out her hand and felt his forehead. He did not object. She realised immediately that the man was feverish. She signalled for a waiter to fetch the bill and helped him to his feet.

'You must lie down immediately. My house is not far off. I don't mind if you accompany me there.'

In a daze he paid the bill, put on his coat and leaned against the woman. His speech was slurred as he talked to her:

'Imagine! A man my age not having ever received a love letter, not even one love letter!'

They walked together past the door covered with a red curtain, and went outside. The street was almost deserted. It appeared desolate as it was buffeted by the onslaught of the rain.

He moaned:

'Someone must love me tonight!'

The tone of his voice indicated that he would soon fall down dead on the wet pavement if no one was prepared to love him that night. He suddenly realised that a woman was standing next to him, so he begged her :

'Love me! Please love me tonight! Don't leave me to die here alone like a rat or an ant or a tortoise! Love me just once. I don't ask you to love me forever. Just love me tonight. Tonight. This night!'

Tears were streaming unashamedly down Abdullah's face. The echo of the drum which had pursued him relentlessly all evening still followed him out into the street. It wasn't singing this time, nor relating stories or fables. It was no longer sending out the message of the African tribe to its lost son. The tribe had long since realised that he had fallen prey to wild animals and was beyond salvation. Hands were furiously pounding on the drum, mourning the lost son and sending bitter weeping which the wind and rain would carry to the far corners of the earth.

10

Lying

I suddenly discovered in myself an amazing talent for lying! Just like that, and without any predetermination, I found myself lying and lying. I turn truths upside down, fabricate with wonderful swiftness the strangest of stories, and tell easily and fluently of events that have not taken place.

The curious thing too is that I tell lies with a courage that comes from I know not where; I don't stutter, get confused or avert my eyes in shame from my interlocutor. I do not sweat or feel the slightest pangs of conscience. I just recite lies as if I am reciting a passage from a Holy Book.

I was the first to be taken by surprise and I stood with amazement, as if witnessing the birth of a miracle. As if it was not I who was speaking; as if this tongue capable of conjuring up lies, a tongue that was all of a sudden put into my mouth; as if it was a strange other and magical person who spoke like this or behaved like that. I was bewildered and unable to explain this amazing power, born of nowhere, a power so compelling that it forced me there and then to change my nature and a whole age of timidity, foolishness, indecisiveness and near-inability to speak. This ease with which I lied made me think that I was mistaken in believing it to be a very complicated and intricate operation which needed a special education and intuitive skills that cannot be simply acquired. One might be born with these skills but they have to be developed through years of practice and experience. I used always to blame myself for a certain village idiocy that stayed with me like my shadow and kept me immobile and unable to achieve any progress either in my quest for living or in my work. I could not seize opportunities and stood by watching my different relatives, nephews, cousins and friends getting on in their jobs, their wages and their influence in society assuming greater proportions. They climbed these magic steps with dizzying speed and were flying in the air while I was tied to the ground with ropes, invisible but heavy and strong like chains. I now know that my village idiocy was indeed heavier than any chains. I was prey to a timidity so over-powering that I did not dare to go to my village. I was afraid of people making comparisons between me and those whom I envied, when we sat together on social occasions. The admiration surrounding them made me disappointed in myself, especially when on leaving I heard the wretched comment:

'Poor thing ... Twenty years in the Civil Service and he still lives in a rented house!'

I used to writhe with pain at this feeling of disappointment, trying to explain it away, dismissing the villagers as naïve and illiterate people who did not know that it was the Devil himself who provided the palaces in which they lived in the city and the vast amounts of money they were so proud of. I even tried explaining to them what I believed in but I met only with stubbornness. 'What you call ''the Devil'',' they stressed, 'is simply the God of luck, intelligence and genius, and what you call honour or honesty, is simply absent-mindedness, idiocy and powerlessness.' And when, out of rage, I found myself trying to point out, as an example, the case of one of the villagers, who grew rich unbelievably quickly by selling fake commodities for merchants, was caught and would be brought to trial, I thought they would denounce him and stone the devil who inspired him to cheat. But no; they gaped with admiration, their eyes glinting with wonder and with handclapping they expressed their joy and merriment at the 'son-of-a-bitch' who 'manifested signs of genius since childhood.'

Damned be the fakery, ignorance, genius, and sons-of-bitches wherever they are. The fault is not the man's or the merchant's. The fault is mine because I am not a genius son-of-a-bitch. I have not yet forged money, taken a bribe, sold fake merchandise, or signed a contract with the Devil. I am simply a contemptuous, jealous, frustrated man, unable to attain the riches others have attained, who, out of sheer powerlessness, labels as aberrations lying, bribery and embezzlement, the successes of others. What makes it worse is that I am trying to forget, and continue to pursue my daily routine. I got to work at the Ministry warehouses, along with the rest, with my eyes cast down so that I see only thousands of plodding feet, thus leaving the sky, stars and high domes for those who possess wings.

Content I was, and should be with the little God offers me. It is at least valid and legal, for I acquire it with effort and hard work and should be able to sleep in comfort, with a clear conscience. But how can I get any rest when my wife, God bless her, keeps a bell under the pillow, which she starts to ring as soon as I come in to sleep. The ringing is so loud that it chases away all the powerful Sultans of sleep.

80

How can I avoid being restless when So-and So managed to build for his family a house with a Paradise-garden (when we hardly manage to pay the rent for miserable accommodation which is nothing but a stable, and when we are pestered by a landlord who is no better than the myrmidons of Hell? This landlord goes so far as to forbid our talking and whispering, and all the time prohibits our children from playing, inventing the silliest reasons to evict us and leave us with nowhere to go). Thoughts like these make the bell's ringing louder.

Not to mention the guy who came back from America with a luxurious car in which he and his family feel as if they are riding in a palace (while we are huddled together in this cave of a house as if we, of all God's creatures, have already given up our share of the sun, air, gardens, rivers and summer resorts).

What about those who send their sons to special schools to learn foreign languages? (I have heard that they teach Chinese in these special schools. China, then, will soon invade the world and our children will meet a black fate, having failed to learn Chinese in a Chinese age. They will surely die of hunger.)

Hundreds of lucky people; the husband who took his wife for a summer holiday in Italy (Oh miserable wife whose bad luck led her to a man who is incapable of taking her for a promenade in the suburbs); the man who celebrates the birthdays of his children by buying them new watches (while our kids have to go through life without watches and will probably die in the street, defenceless without watches).

And so on and so forth; the bell continues to ring night after night, setting me tossing about, sleepless, my head full of scorpions, dogs, snakes, palaces, languages, gardens, watches, terror, damnation and death. Sometimes I die, see myself with my neck in chains, being dragged to hell by its ruffianly myrmidons. 'This is a mistake' I shout in protest. 'I'm one of the Paradise crowd! I lived my life in all honesty and truthfulness. I did not lie, steal or cheat, a breadcrumb is all I wanted.' But my protestations of innocence are in vain, for they fling me into the air towards the flaming pits. The fiery burning of my body wakens me, and I come back to life terrified and start praying to God to give me some of his immense forgiveness and goodness. And then it is time to go to work, whereupon I find myself seated at my scorched table and there in the warehouse I bury my head in papers, folders and registration cards. Ten years I have been working here and it never occurred to me once to look up to see what kind of ceiling I was working under!

To be sure, I am not totally ignorant of the rules of dealing with people. I might say something out of politeness and courtesy, something that I do not really mean. I might check myself and refrain from saying something, again out of politeness, timidity or fear, and I might pretend to be happy sometimes, or sad, according to the demands of ethics. I might follow the others in adopting an easygoing attitude toward my superiors and hard-headed influential people, to avoid their anger. These were the boundaries outside of which I would be helpless and would drown in the shallowest of water, being as I was, unable to make up one imaginary story. Even if I tried, I would stutter, tremble and sweat, and before long would betray myself and come right out with the truth, regardless that this might lead to being fired. All this explains why I was astonished to discover that I am explosively capable of telling lies.

I was at the time running down the street to do some chores. Someone I knew took hold of my arm. He was expecting me to do him a favour, so he overwhelmed me with the warmest and most prolonged greetings. I was feeling a strange kind of melancholy, a heavy sort of depression in my breast. As soon as he broached his subject I told him, impatiently: 'I'm going home shortly ... phone me!'

I knew for certain that I was not going home shortly and of course I did not have a telephone.

'What is the number?'

I managed on the spur of the moment to invent a number. I did not hesitate, turn my eyes from his or feel the slightest pang of regret or bad conscience. I simply told him, bade him farewell and went on my way. It dawned on me that I had performed a spontaneous act from the start, an act which took me some time to understand. I stood in the middle of the street with a sense of astonishment, contemplating what had happened and wondering at what I had actually said. At that moment I was taken by a sweeping desire to laugh. All the clouds of melancholy pressing on my heart were evaporated to make way for the rains of joy. Straightaway, half-believing, I proceeded to practise my newly-acquired skill. I went into the shop of a merchant who acted as an import agent for the ministry store. I found myself completely occupied fabricating stories about my relations with senior officials. I told him that I would ask them to give him a position of merit in their business and that he could expect a big deal. The man, understandably enough, left his customers to concentrate on me. He ordered coffee to be brought for me, but I alleged that I had an urgent appointment with the Ministry Under-Secretary, and left.

I was so happy with myself that I wondered whether I was under the spell of a caprice arising out of my feeling of depression. Nevertheless I continued to seize any opportunity to try out my new aptitude.

'What is the time please?'

'I don't have a watch.'

It did not matter whether he saw my wrist-watch or not. All I cared about was the chance and my ability to say what I wanted to say. I was extremely happy, just like a person who, reaching the age of puberty, suddenly discovers he can perform the sexual act.

'Is this the way to the National Bank?'

He was mistakably going in the right direction. But what harm would it do if I made him lose his way for a bit?

'No, it's in the other direction.'

Just like that, gratuitous lying for the fun and practice of it. Even the next day, when I met my colleagues at work, my appetite for lying was still of the strongest.

'May I borrow your pen for a minute?'

'I don't have a pen.'

No matter how trivial the subject, and no matter how many pens I happened to have in my drawer or in my jacket pocket I would lie, taking into consideration that I had, during my past idiocy, lost numerous pens, some valuable, simply because I had rushed to hand them over. Now I really admire my way of pronouncing my lying words. I am so self-assured and so confident, that the person asking would believe me even though he saw me carrying twenty pens.

And so I went on seizing every opportunity and occasion to exercise this invisible and magical muscle that had lain dormant in me and was unnoticeable until recently, a muscle that had been lying asleep and neglected. I shall now make up for all those years of neglect and idleness, and I shall over-use it to the maximum. I continue to lie, lie and lie, at work and outside work to my colleagues, the customers and my superiors, at home, and abroad. Let everything I say be lies, let this newly-discovered muscle grow, gain in immunity and strength. It does not matter if people detect my lies. I do not care about their approval or disapproval, for actually I do not lie to achieve any interest or aim. I have no intention in mind. It is all for the sheer fun and games of it, a simple exercise for a muscle that all of a sudden came to life.

Little by little, new worlds opened up; everything around me became exciting, and I broke away from that monotonous orbit that had been my life, that deadly routine which made my days neglected and dull replies of each other. I now behold my world; every day new stories, experiences and adventures. Interest is centred on me, battles are waged because of me. A man of no importance has become suddenly the centre of universal attention. What an incredible transformation in a man's life! Furthermore, I have become convinced that lying is the rule and truth-telling the exception, that what is beautiful is so because it is deceitful. Only because the newsreels are lies and exaggerations do we listen; it is only because the newspapers are a mass of fabrication that we read them. Not to mention literature that arouses people's feelings and gains glory and immortality for the authors. Is it not all lying? Is it not the sheer trumping up of stories and myths, that have no realistic weight? It is beautiful only because it is lies.

Take the sparrows; they sing lies and thus enchant us. Take spring; it would not be the most beautiful of all the seasons if it were not the most deceitful. The same goes for views of sunrise and sunset; they are beautiful because they are deceitful. Even the stars which we see filling the sky with beauty – are they not immense and awesome planets, some of which have disappeared millions of years ago? What about the sun? Is it not a huge planet that does not change its position? I dare say that everything we see and admire is lies; even the most beautiful of women is false and the cleverest at sugar-coating, cheating, and hiding her true nature. Oh how beautiful I am when lying!

Lying is as easy for me as eating, drinking and breathing. I like to lie and lie and find no other happiness and enjoyment than in lying. I do not stutter and tremble. I feel ashamed only when I find myself in a position where I have to tell the truth. I do not know how lying made me grow two wings with which I soar high into the air like a bird of prey. I do not know how my circle of friends widened – people flock around me as if I am the provider of feasts not the purveyor of lies – how day by day this circle grows, to include all the influential people in our society, those who until recently I could see only from a distance and whom I regarded with respect and fear; or how, suddenly, they became the dearest of friends, my companions far into the night, on outings, and in travelling.

Moreover, I do not know how I moved from that damp store to an office on an upper floor with windows and decorative balconies, or how I left my old house in one of the poorest quarters of town to live in a house with a garden, next to the sea. Or how I managed to form my own company, to get involved in exchange, deals, international tenders, with secretaries addressing me in foreign languages which miraculously I began to understand, and to talk and negotiate with businessmen in the world capitals. It has become clear to me that all those who reach this new world are masters of deceit; that my only challenge when dealing with them is to outsmart them with bigger and extremely skilful lies. For there is still lying more refined, more beautiful and more polished than that already stated. Nothing but lying, lying and lying; my master, my patron, my benefactor; lying …His Majesty Lying!